D

Sophie could hear ━━━━━ the living-room and sh━━━━━━━━ne. There was a strange ━━━━━ and it wasn't the maid's cheap perfume. This was a richer, wilder smell, like the smell of freshly-turned earth when a new grave was dug.

"Yolanda, will you come here for a minute!" she cried, "I've got something to tell you—"

She stopped short at the entrance to the living room. It wasn't the maid but it was certainly someone Sophie knew very well indeed.

And for a terrible unthinking second, Sophie smiled with delight. It was Jeff, and he had come to see her.

And then she remembered.

"It can't be you," she breathed. "You're . . . you're dead . . ."

"That's right, sweetheart," came the mocking reply. "And now so are you."

BOOKS IN THE *HORROR HIGH*
SERIES AVAILABLE FROM
BOXTREE

HORROR HIGH

Demon Brood

Nigel Robinson

B⬢XTREE

First published in Great Britain in 1994 by BOXTREE
LIMITED, Broadwall House, 21 Broadwall, London SE1 9PL

10 9 8 7 6 5 4 3 2 1

ISBN: 1 85283 363 7

Cover artwork © Paul Campion
Phototypeset by Intype, London
Printed and bound in Great Britain by
Cox & Wyman Ltd, Reading, Berkshire

A CIP catalogue entry for this book is available from the
British Library

Prologue

Sophie Ashford threw her schoolbooks down onto the bed and sighed with relief. It had been a particularly hard week at Castlemare High and now she was looking forward to the weekend.

Her parents were away, called off on a last-minute business trip to New York. That was probably just as well, she realised, as it meant that they wouldn't find out that she'd failed mid-term exams in cruddy old Mr Chippenham's chemistry class.

After all, they had spent thousands upon thousands of pounds sending her to one of the top fee-paying schools in the country and it wouldn't do for them to find out that their darling daughter was getting a steady string of D-minuses in her A-level classes.

Still, what did it matter, she asked herself as she sat down at her dressing table and examined her face in the vanity mirror, giving it the same sort of attention that her fellow chemistry students would give to a complex polymer chain. Who cared about A-level grades when you were as pretty as this?

With her long dark hair and her flawlessly white complexion, as white as that of a china doll's, Sophie knew she was a stunner. She was also well aware that half the boys at Castlemare would willingly sacrifice their boring old B-pluses to go out with her. With looks like this, she'd have all the jetsetting playboys with their pots of cash lining up for her as soon as she had taken—and possibly even failed—her A-levels!

Damn! Another zit!

Sophie cursed under her breath as she examined the offending blemish in the mirror. That really upset her; in fact, in terms of disaster it ranked somewhere near her £250-a-week allowance being stopped by her parents.

She walked over to the window of her bedroom and looked out. It was mid-October and already the dark and rainy nights were drawing in. Outside her bedroom window she could see the great Victorian cemetery of Highgate, standing out like a huge black blot amid all the twinkling lights and flashy mansions of wealthy North London.

Sophie shuddered. The school had organised a guided tour there once, visiting the mausoleums and tombs of the great and the famous, and she'd found that the place had given her a major case of the creeps. And that had been in broad daylight: heaven help anyone crazy enough to visit there at night!

The only advantage to living so near the cemetery, Sophie decided, was its proximity to school. She could walk there—or more usually jog—instead of driving through the horrendous early-morning traffic in her brand-new Porsche, the one her industrialist father had bought her last year for her seventeenth birthday.

Sophie decided that she needed some serious cheering up. She had the entire house to herself for the weekend and, when Sophie Ashford had the entire house to herself, then that meant a party. She took a sheet of paper and her Montblanc fountain pen out of her schoolbag, and started to make a list of all the people she'd invite.

There was Calvin Charles, of course. He was quite a cutie, even if he was an American, and—who knows?—after a few glasses of her father's fine red wine he might even take a fancy to her. Peter Armitage would have to come as well, of course; he wasn't exactly God's gift, but his dad did work for the BBC and that was bound to come in handy if she found herself needing a job when she left Castlemare High. Maybe dishy Nick Dent too, if she could tear him away from his work on the school's student newspaper.

And then, of course, there was Jeff . . .

Sophie slammed her left hand down hard on the dressing table, annoyed at her mistake.

There is no Jeff! she reminded herself angrily. *Not any more! He's gone! Gone for good!*

She took a deep breath and returned to her list. Reluctantly she realised that she'd have to invite some girls along as well; otherwise it would look like the party was being set up primarily for Sophie Ashford to find herself a new boyfriend (which, of course, it was).

Bernadette Murphy, of course. She and Sophie weren't exactly the best of friends, but at least the feisty Irish girl was interesting and could be relied upon to keep the more nerdy boys occupied; and, what was more, she wasn't pretty enough to pose any real threat to Sophie.

Kim Nishida too: her father might have just won the Nobel Prize but the Anglo-Japanese girl was so dizzy and dippy that, next to her, even Sophie would appear sophisticated and intelligent.

She'd draw the line at Francesca Barton though: the last time Sophie and the glamorous flame-haired chemistry student had been at a party together they'd started arguing—over Jeff, of course. They'd finished the evening off by pouring expensive red wine down each other's white designer dresses. Sophie's dress had been stained so much that her father had had to buy her a new one the following day. Sophie couldn't understand why he was so upset; it had only cost him £700 after all.

Sophie had just finished drawing up her list and was about to go to the telephone to arrange for an outside caterer when she heard the front door click open downstairs.

She sighed. It was typical of Yolanda, their Portugese maid. She was always forgetting something and having to come back to collect it; she'd have to have a word with her about that—she couldn't have her unexpectedly turning up in the middle of her party tomorrow night. Who knew what might be going on—if she got lucky!

"Yolanda, is that you?" she asked, standing at the head of the stairs.

No reply. Sophie's parents had bought Yolanda a portable stereo for her birthday a few months ago and the young Portugese woman seemed to spend most of her time these days permanently plugged into the latest trendy and sexy boy-band.

Sophie could hear Yolanda clunking around in the living-room and she ran down the stairs two at a time. There was a strange smell in the air, Sophie noticed, and it certainly wasn't the Portugese maid's cheap perfume. This was a richer, wilder smell, like the smell of freshly turned earth when a new grave was dug.

"Yolanda, will you turn that thing off for a minute!" she cried. "I've got something to tell you—"

She stopped short at the entrance to the living-room. It wasn't Yolanda—but it certainly was some-one Sophie knew very well indeed.

And for a terrible, unthinking second Sophie smiled with delight.

And then she remembered.

"What—what are you doing here?"

"Hello, sweetheart, it's nice to see you again."

The voice was cracked and dull, and there was an unearthly *coldness* about it.

Sophie wanted to turn and run, but her legs wouldn't move as the figure approached her. Her eyes were flooded with tears of joy—and tears of sheer unbelieving horror as well.

"It can't be . . ." she gasped.

"Ooooh, sweetheart, you don't know how much I've missed you. It's been a long, long time . . ."

Sophie's lips quivered, but no sound would come from her mouth. The figure came nearer, and that smell of damp earth was stronger now.

And there was another smell too, one that made Sophie want to throw up.

The heavy, stomach-turning, putrid stink of decaying flesh.

The figure was face-to-face with her now, looking down at her with blank, unseeing eyes. His breath smelt vile and rotten, making her want to gag.

Finally Sophie found her voice.

"It can't be you," she breathed. "You're . . . you're dead . . ."

"That's right, sweetheart," came the mocking reply. "And now so are you."

Chapter 1

"Vampires!"

Kim Nishida licked her lips with relish, and waved her arms around like Dracula preparing to swoop down on an unsuspecting victim. Several people in the senior common room looked in amusement at the petite half-Japanese girl, before returning to their own business. But then, with her way-out clothes and urchin hairdo, Kim always did have the reputation of being a bit wacky and eccentric. Someone had once described her as looking like a Japanese version of Kate Bush in one of her dafter videos, and Kim had actually taken it as a compliment.

"I tell you," she repeated, "it has to be vampires!"

"Perverts," stated Bernadette Murphy confidently, and Kim's face fell. She indicated the front page of the *Castlemare Gazette*, the school's own student newspaper.

"Then how do you account for this, Murphy?" she demanded. "Graves in Highgate Cemetery being disturbed—desecrated even?"

"Vandals, sick kids out for kicks," came Murphy's flat reply. "There's nothing weird or supernatural out a few graves being destroyed in a cemetery, Kim. In all probability it's just a couple of boys from Castlemare who've got bored playing around with their parents' credit cards and wanted to try something different."

Kim sulked. "Sometimes I think you're far too down-to-earth, Murphy."

"I have to be," Murphy smiled, and threw back her long blonde hair. "I'm an A-level science student—I deal in facts, not fantasy!"

Kim stuck her tongue out at her best friend.

"But this is fact!" she insisted, revelling in her theory. "There have always been tales of vampires lurking in Highgate Cemetery. Lost spirits rising from their graves at night to spread fear and terror throughout the rich suburbs of North London!"

"Lost spirits?" scoffed Murphy. "Spirits of another kind if you ask me!"

"Well, I didn't!" Kim giggled, and then another even wilder thought struck her. "Hey, maybe it's bodysnatchers. You know, hard-up students selling off the corpses to the local hospital for a hefty profit!"

Murphy couldn't help but laugh. " 'Hard-up students'? Here, at Castlemare?"

"Well, it's an idea . . ."

"We're students at one of the most exclusive schools in the country,"

Murphy reminded her. "Your dad's a Nobel Prize-winner; back home in Ireland, my mum's just been named Businesswoman of the Year. The students at Castlemare are the sons and daughters of millionaire financiers, rock stars and inter-

8

national politicians. We're all about as hard-up as Madonna at the end of a world tour!"

"With a little more good taste, I would hope?"

The two girls turned to see Francesca Barton, the red-headed heartbreaker of the sixth form. As usual she was wearing the latest colourful and figure-hugging Versace creation which showed off to the best advantage her more than adequate vital statistics.

"Of course," said Murphy, suddenly feeling very dowdy next to Francesca, dressed as she was in a sloppy sweatshirt and jeans. "We were just talking about the vandalism in Highgate Cemetery." She showed Francesca the front page of the *Gazette*. "It's sick, disturbing the dead like that."

"That's right," agreed Francesca, with a note of regret. "The dead should be allowed to rest in peace."

Kim caught the sadness in their friend's voice. "I'm sorry, Frannie, we forgot . . ."

Francesca brushed a tear away from her eye. "It's OK, Kim, I'm getting over it now."

"You still miss him, huh?" Even Murphy was being sympathetic now.

Francesca shrugged. "Who wouldn't? Everyone liked him—even mum and dad gave him a key to our house. Jeff was the kindest, sweetest, most charming guy I've ever known."

"And the best-looking too," added Murphy.

"You bet!" piped up Kim lasciviously. "I tell you, half the girls at Castlemare would have sold their own grandmothers to get into his—"

9

She shut up suddenly as Murphy kicked her in the shin.

"Sorry," Kim said. "I'm not exactly known for my tact . . ."

Francesca smiled. It was no secret that her ex-boyfriend, Jeff Rawlinson, had generally been regarded by most of the girls as the prize catch at Castlemare High.

After all, when a guy's six-feet-three, with steel-blue eyes and the cutest smile this side of Tom Cruise—and has the sort of gym-trained physique that by the age of seventeen had had him advertising jeans on TV—then he's bound to enjoy a reputation as the school hunk. With, as Kim had said, all the girls after him, it was a wonder that he and Francesca had gone out together for as long as they had.

But now Jeff was gone, and Francesca was learning how to live life without him.

"Don't worry, Kim," Francesca said bravely. "Life goes on." She changed the subject: "So, what's all this about bodysnatchers?"

"Or vampires," Murphy added mischievously. "Kim thinks that Count Dracula's checked into town. The next thing you know it'll be an outbreak of Egyptian mummies!"

"You both think I'm being superstitious and silly, don't you?" Kim said defensively.

"Yes," agreed Murphy, but not unkindly.

Kim scowled at her. "In my country, back in Japan, we know there are more things in heaven or Earth—"

"—'than are dreamt of in your philosohy'," Francesca completed the Shakespeare quote for her. "You've been doing your homework, Kim."

Nonplussed, Kim continued: "And, after all, we are approaching Hallowe'en . . ."

"You mean October thirty-first," Murphy pointed out in her infuriatingly no-nonsense tone of voice.

"*Hallowe'en*," repeated Kim firmly. "And we all know what happens then—"

"Most terrifying date of the year," Murphy shuddered. "Chemistry homework's due in."

"No!" said Kim, exasperated. "The forces of darkness are let loose on the world," she went on dramatically. "The dead will rise from their graves . . ."

Murphy and Francesca looked at her, singularly unimpressed, as the bell rang, indicating the start of afternoon classes. Kim laughed, and then began to collect her books.

"Don't say I didn't warn you!" she said jokingly. "When the clock strikes midnight and there's a tapping at your door . . ."

"Go to your class, Kim!" Murphy urged.

"OK, OK, OK," she said. "I'll see you boring old non-believers later. You still on for tonight?"

"Try and stop us," said Francesca. "There's only one place to be on Monday nights."

She waved goodbye to the Japanese girl, who left the common room. When she had gone, Murphy turned to Francesca.

"Would you believe it?" she said in amazement. "Kim actually believes all that nonsense!"

"Who's to say she's not right?" asked Francesca thoughtfully.

Murphy groaned. "Not you as well!"

"I don't believe in witches and warlocks and all that stuff," Francesca began.

"Well, that's a relief then. I was beginning to think that I was the only sane person left at Castlemare."

"But she's right about the cemetery," Francesca continued. "There have always been legends of vampires and bodysnatchers there. Ever since the place opened in 1839."

"I'm surprised you know that."

Francesca shrugged. "Jeff's buried there," she reminded her.

"That's something that's bothered me," said Murphy. "I thought they no longer buried people at Highgate Cemetery."

"He was interred in the family plot," explained Francesca. "His family have owned it since the early 1850s."

Murphy nodded. She knew how difficult it must be for Francesca to talk about her dead ex-boyfriend. When Jeff had started seeing Francesca it had seemed to everyone at Castlemare that he had finally found his soulmate. Francesca had been devastated when she learnt only two and a half months ago that Jeff had died of a rare blood condition.

"Kim didn't upset you, did she?" asked Murphy. "With all her talk of vampires and bodysnatchers?"

Francesca laughed. "She's got a vivid imagination, that's all," she said. "She takes after her father."

"He did win the Nobel Prize for Literature last year," Murphy agreed, then added, "Not that that should impress you—after all, your mum's pretty famous too . . ."

Francesca shrugged nonchalantly. "Nobel Prize for Science? Mum got that three years ago through doing some boring research on micro-enzymes—I couldn't get interested in them if my life depended on it! All she got out of that was several thousands of dollars which went towards her research and a round-the-world trip for the family."

"A free holiday's not bad," said Murphy. "When Mum was voted Businesswoman of the Year, all we got was an increased tax demand from the Inland Revenue!"

Francesca laughed sympathetically. "In that case, Murphy, the sushi's on me tonight!"

"You bet!"

"The French have spent hundreds of years perfecting the fine art of *haute cuisine*," complained Calvin Charles as he poked at his food with a pair of chopsticks, "and what do the Japanese come up with—" he waved a piece of food in Kim's face, to make his point—"raw fish!"

"It's called sushi, you idiot!" giggled Kim. "And it's supposed to be trendy!"

"That's all right then," he agreed, and popped a bite-sized piece of abalone into his mouth. "If it's trendy then I'm all for it!"

Every Monday night Tokyo Joe's Sushi Bar was

packed with students from Castlemare High, who came there for the easy, laid-back ambiance, the delicious and reasonably priced food, and the fact that the Japanese proprietor turned a blind eye when they ordered bottles of wine or sake, even though most of them were still under eighteen.

It was also one of the hippest places to go in North London, and, as Tokyo Joe himself had taken a particular shine to Kim and her friends, the portions he gave them were invariably large and exceptionally delicious.

"What I don't understand," continued Calvin in his New York accent, wiping a spot of soy sauce off his white Katharine Hamnett shirt, "is why we don't all drop down dead from food poisoning. After all, it can't be healthy eating all this uncooked food."

"Your stomach's made of cast-iron," quipped Murphy, remembering the last Christmas party when Calvin had drunk more than his fair share of red wine and eaten half a Christmas cake all by himself. Somehow he'd still managed to stagger home with his good looks and that cute little black kiss-curl intact. "It'd take more than uncooked fish to knock you for six!"

"Everything's fresh," explained Kim. "As if it had just been taken out of the sea five minutes ago."

"Fresh?" Calvin scoffed. "This is London. You might not have noticed, but the nearest bit of sea's over fifty miles away!"

"Aha! But if you were to look in the back you'd see that Joe keeps salt-water tanks full of live fish which he takes out when he needs to."

Murphy pulled a face and looked down at her own bowl of sushi. "So you mean that what I'm eating now was alive about five minutes ago . . ." she said slowly.

"That's right," said Kim cheerfully, and munched on a piece of fish.

Francesca went a distinct shade of green. "I feel sick," she said. "My dad's got an aquarium at home—and if I thought that those fish were swimming around in there just waiting to be eaten . . ."

Kim laughed. "Lighten up, Frannie!" she chuckled. "Like I said, it's trendy. And what's more, it's healthy!"

"And just how do you make that out?" Murphy asked.

"The Japanese have one of the lowest incidences of heart disease in the world," Kim explained. "And raw fish forms a large part of our diet."

"Well, I've heard horror stories about people dying from eating sushi," Frannie said doubtfully, remembering the back copies of the *Sunday Sport* or the *National Enquirer* her dad loved to read when her mother wasn't looking.

"It all depends what you eat, and how you prepare the food," Kim continued, clearly enjoying talking about the cuisine of her own country. "Eat the wrong sort of fish, like the puffer fish, for example, and—"

"And what?" Francesca was interested in spite of herself.

Kim dragged a finger across her neck and made

a croaking sound. "It's one of the most poisonous fish around. You'd be dead in minutes."

Murphy winced. "Whatever happened to good old British cooking with meat and two veg?" she asked.

Calvin patted her sympathetically on the back. "This is Castlemare High, Murphy, we've got more nationalities here than the United Nations!"

"That's impossible," she pointed out, but couldn't suppress a smile. Calvin did have a typical American tendency towards exaggeration.

"Well, almost," he grinned, accentuating that cute little dimple in his chin which he knew drove all the girls wild. "Just look around this table. English, Irish, American, Japanese. Hey, tomorrow we've even got someone coming in from the Caribbean!"

Francesca beamed. "I spent a wonderful summer holiday there once . . ."

"The Caribbean?" asked Murphy. She always liked to be up with the latest gossip but this was news even to her.

"From Haiti," Calvin explained and took a card from the back pocket of his Levi's. "Some guy called—" he read the name on the card "—Jean-Pierre Denfer. A diplomat's son, apparently, just like me. He's been in London for about a month now, but this will be his first week at Castlemare."

"And just how do you know so much about him?" Murphy asked.

"I've been assigned to look after him during his first few days at school, make sure he doesn't feel too lonely," Calvin said glumly. "Can you imagine it? Heck, his island was under American occupation until 1941! He's gonna love me!"

"I think he's going to be fascinating," Kim decided. "He'll be able to tell us all about life on Haiti, all its customs . . ."

"Customs?" asked Francesca, confused, but Murphy could see what her best friend was leading to.

"Voodoo!" she said, and laughed. "There you go, Kim, at last you'll have someone to swap spells with!"

Chapter 2

"*Enchanté, mademoiselle Bernadette*," said Jean-Pierre the following day and bent down to kiss her outstretched hand, as a cavalier would do in an old movie.

Calvin raised his eyes heavenwards—really this guy was so straight it was unbelievable!—but Murphy giggled, enormously impressed by the young Haitian's old-world charm.

"Charmed, I'm sure," she said in what Calvin had often called her best "Duchess" voice, "but please call me Murphy, like everyone else. I hate Bernadette."

"Then Murphy it shall be," he declaimed in his heavy French accent. "And you shall call me Jean-Pierre."

"Pleased to meet you, Jean-Pierre," she said, and eyed him appreciatively.

Jean-Pierre's father was a native Haitian, but his mother was French and Jean-Pierre combined the best of both races. With his dusky skin, brooding good looks and casually understated clothes, Murphy bet that he'd soon be attracting the attention of most of the girls in the upper school.

She looked over at Calvin, whose eyes were

practically glowing green with jealousy; ever since Jeff's death he'd liked thinking of himself as the official Castlemare hunk: now it seemed as if Jean-Pierre might offer some very serious competition.

"It is indeed a great honour to be allowed to attend Castlemare, Murphy," Jean-Pierre said in his curiously stylised English.

"I'm sure your dad's cheque had something to do with it," said Calvin, more sarcastically than he had intended. Murphy shot him a look which said, *Shut up, will you!*

"And I hope that I shall be worthy of the faith placed in me," Jean-Pierre continued.

"Castlemare must be a change from the Caribbean," said Murphy as she took his arm and led him to the window of the senior common room. Outside the rain was coming down in sheets and a fierce October wind was howling through the oak, beech and yew trees which lined the courtyard.

"*Bien sûr,*" agreed Jean-Pierre, "I have never seen it rain so many dogs and cats before."

"Cats and dogs," Murphy pleasantly corrected him, while, behind them, Calvin let out a silent guffaw.

Boy! he thought. *Does this geek ever have a lot to learn! Maybe he's not gonna be so much competition after all!*

"I see that I have a lot to learn," Jean-Pierre smiled. "I must improve my English here—"

"Whatever for?" asked Murphy, and shot a sweet-as-poison look at Calvin. "Calvin's from New York and he's never tried to improve his."

Calvin considered sticking his tongue out at

his friend, decided it was incredibly childish, then did it anyway.

Jean-Pierre laughed. "The English humour, English manners, English ways. If I am to study at Castlemare then I must behave like an English schoolboy."

"I wouldn't start doing that until Kim gets to meet you," said Calvin, and even Murphy smiled.

"Kim? Who is Kim?"

"Kim's our resident white witch!" Calvin said fliply.

"Kim is not our 'resident white witch'," Murphy corrected him frostily. "She just happens to be interested in the occult, that's all."

"And is she ever looking forward to meeting you, Jean-Pierre, my man," continued Calvin. "She's tried Tarot cards, crystal balls, rune stones and all the rest of that mumbo-jumbo. Now she reckons that it's about time she did a spot of voodoo!"

"Do not speak of the religion of my ancestors like that!" Jean-Pierre suddenly snapped. Calvin and Murphy were both surprised by the Haitian's ferocity.

Calvin raised his hands defensively. "Hey, man, I'm sorry," he said, and meant it. "I didn't mean to upset you."

Jean-Pierre waved aside his apology. "You are an American, you would not be expected to understand," he said, carefully hiding the anger in his voice. "But you must not speak ill of the gods of voodoo or else I cannot be held responsible for the consequences . . ."

There was an awkward silence, broken only by

the sound of the rain as it continued to pound away at the window-pane. Finally Calvin spoke up.

"Look, Jean-Pierre, I really am sorry," he said again. "It's just that I thought voodoo was nothing more than an old superstition—you know, something along the lines of vampires and rabbits' feet, and not walking under ladders."

Jean-Pierre shook his head sadly. "Voodoo is not a superstition, Calvin, it is as real as anything here at Castlemare. It is nothing less than a fully-fledged religion with its own gods—and its own devils.

"I am a Christian, as are most of my countrymen, but we have all come to learn to respect the ancient laws of voodoo. Talk disrespectfully of the spirits of our dead ancestors, mock Baron Samedi, or the great Lord Damballah, and all Hell can—and will—break loose . . ."

Calvin and Murphy shivered: it had suddenly become very cold indeed.

During the lunchbreak Kim and Francesca took shelter from the rain in the gazebo in the middle of Castlemare's great lawn which stretched down to Hampstead Heath. Kim was picking at a takeaway which had just been brought to the school by the cute delivery boy at Tokyo Joe's; Francesca, even more mindful of her slim figure than her friend, was munching away at the fifty-three calories of her apple.

Calvin came running up the lawn to them, sloshing through the mud and holding his Aviator leather jacket high above his head to protect himself from the rain.

"Well, have you seen him?" asked Kim as he threw himself down on the bench beside them.

"Seen who?"

"Jean-Pierre, of course."

"Oh yeah, the Voodoo King," said Calvin off-handedly.

Francesca grinned. "Aha! Do I detect the little green god of jealousy, Calvin?"

"What d'you mean?"

Francesca turned to Kim and adopted an all-girls-together attitude. "From what I hear, Jean-Pierre is one major hunk. Which means that our Calvin here is going to have his work cut out now chasing the girls."

"Hey, there's more than enough of you to go around,' Calvin said. "Why should I worry?"

Francesca ignored this remark and continued her gentle teasing.

"You hate competition, Calvin!" she laughed. "That's why you and Jeff never got on! He beat you in getting that contract—"

Calvin shrugged. The two of them had been up for a starring role in a TV commercial for designer jeans. It had been no contest: Jeff with his classic model looks had walked the boards with Calvin.

"So I wasn't as pretty-boy as he was . . ." he said dismissively, although it was obvious that Francesca had struck a raw nerve.

"And he always beat you in getting the girls!" she continued.

Calvin regarded Francesca through narrow, resentful eyes. "At least when I'm going with a girl, I stay steady with her for longer than two or three weeks," he said. "I seem to recall he dumped you pretty quickly—what was it, four weeks?"

Francesca turned quickly away, and there was the suspicion of a tear in her eyes. By her side Kim glowered at Calvin.

Calvin put a comforting arm around Francesca's shoulder.

"Hey, look, sweetheart, I'm sorry," he said softly. "It's just my big mouth running way out of line again. I know how much you cared for him."

Francesca turned to him. "I really do miss him, you know," she sobbed. "Even after we split up I still cared for him a lot . . ."

Calvin cradled her head in his hands. "I know, sweetheart, I know." Kim kept quiet: she'd also been out with Jeff, although they'd managed to keep it a secret, and Francesca certainly didn't know.

Calvin turned Francesca's face towards his and looked at her with his big brown puppy-dog eyes, giving her the sort of look he knew from experience could melt any girl's heart.

"Am I forgiven?" he asked.

Francesca nodded, and Calvin gave her an affectionate and brotherly kiss on the cheek. Suddenly he felt Kim tugging at the sleeve of his shirt.

She pointed to the police car which was slowly pulling up the drive towards the main Castlemare building. The figure of the Principal, Miss Greystone, was waiting for the two police officers as they got out of the squad car. She was dressed all in black, and was standing under an umbrella in the pouring rain.

"What's going on?" asked Francesca.

"They're coming to take Miss Greystone away?" Kim suggested hopefully.

"Let's find out!" said Calvin and took each girl by the hand and ran up the hill to the school building.

"A heart attack!" gasped Murphy, and shook her head. She had met Calvin, Francesca and Kim as they were walking down the steps from the main school building, and she couldn't believe what they had just told her.

"That's what we heard," said Calvin, who, along with Francesca and Kim, had been eavesdropping at the Principal's study door while Miss Greystone spoke to the police. "It must have happened over the weekend sometime. The Portuguese maid had a day off yesterday so she didn't find her until today."

"But she was only seventeen!" Murphy protested. "People don't have heart attacks at our age!"

"Well, Sophie did," said Kim.

"At first the police thought she might have surprised a burglar," Calvin continued. "Some of her things were disturbed; but there was no sign of a break-in so they've put it down to natural causes."

"So there'll be no post-mortem then?" asked Francesca.

"No."

Francesca shuddered. "That poor girl, all alone in that big house with no one to turn to. It must have been horrible for her . . ." She fell silent for

24

a moment and then asked Calvin, "When did they say the burial was going to be?"

"They didn't," Calvin said. "Sophie's not going to be buried—she's going to be cremated. She had this phobia about being buried alive."

Francesca shuddered once again and, for a second, there was look of horror of her face.

"Are you OK, Frannie?" Calvin asked, his voice full of concern.

"The thought of fire," she said. "It must be horrible, being burnt like that."

"Sophie's dead, Frannie," Murphy said softly. "She won't feel a thing."

Francesca gave a little laugh. "Of course not," she said. "I forgot for a moment, that's all . . ."

Calvin nodded over to Jean-Pierre who was approaching them, carrying a pile of books under his arm.

"Here comes the Voodoo King," he said.

"The Hunk, you mean," Francesca said huskily, and sniggered as she saw Calvin start to splutter with rage. It would do the young New Yorker good to realise that he wasn't the only cute boy at Castlemare, she thought.

Jean-Pierre came up to them and Murphy introduced him to the two other girls. He kissed them both on the hand as he had with Murphy earlier that day. When he was introduced to Kim, he smiled knowingly.

"Ah yes, 'the white witch' of Castlemare, I believe Calvin called you!" he said mischievously.

"Calvin, you didn't!" Kim was outraged.

"Hey, it was only a joke!"

"The ways of voodoo are no joke, Miss Nishida," Jean-Pierre said sombrely. "You flout them at your peril."

Kim frowned: she had the feeling that she was being put very much in her place. Suddenly Jean-Pierre seemed much wiser and older than his seventeen years.

"It is not like your fortune-telling cards, or your star signs in the newspaper," he continued. "They're simply parlour games to pass the time of day. Voodoo is a serious religion, as real as Christianity or Buddhism. Study it if you like; but beware that the forces you may conjure into existence you may not be able to control . . ."

Calvin put up a hand to silence the young Haitian. "Whoa, Jean-Pierre," he said. "Give it a rest, will you? We're all spooked enough as it is!"

"*Vraiment*? And why is that?" he asked, and Murphy told him of Sophie's death. "Then she has gone to join her *loas*," he said.

"Her what?" Calvin had the strangest feeling that he'd just stepped into a late-night horror movie.

"Her *loas*, her ancestor-gods," Jean-Pierre explained. "She will be happy with them. You say that she is to be cremated?"

"That's right." Francesca nodded.

"Then she's doubly fortunate, and may rest in peace," he smiled. "Not even the greatest obeah in the world can turn a pile of ash into one of the walkers."

Calvin, Murphy, Kim and Francesca all exchanged mystified looks. Jean-Pierre looked at his watch—an expensive Rolex, given to him by his father for his sixteenth birthday.

"I must go," he said.

"But Jean-Pierre, it's still lunchtime," said Francesca. "You're welcome to spend the rest of it with us."

Jean-Pierre smiled but shook his head, and indicated the pile of books under his arm. "I have come to Castlemare to study," he said, somehwat prissily, thought Calvin "I will do that in the school library. My grades are not very good: it is important that I improve on them."

Francesca shrugged as if to say: *OK, have it your own way then*, and waved him goodbye. After he had left Calvin turned to the girls.

"He's a weirdo, and that's no mistake!" he chuckled.

"He wants good grades," countered Murphy. "You should take a leaf out of his book!"

"And he's still a hunk," Francesca added, just to annoy Calvin even more. "But what was all that stuff about 'obeah' and 'the walkers'?"

"You're the expert on mumbo-jumbo, Kim," Calvin said. "What did he mean?"

"I don't know," said Kim. "And you know something—I don't think I *want* to know either . . ."

Kim spent a worried night at home in her parents' house in a pretty side road just off Hampstead Heath. Jean-Pierre's sudden outburst earlier that day had disturbed her, and she realised that up to now her fascination with the occult had been nothing more than a foolish schoolgirl fad.

It was great fun to think that there were greater forces at work in the universe, forces which controlled our destinies, and made tomorrow's maths homework or the D-minus she received in French conversation the previous week fade into insignificance.

Her interest was also partly a reaction against her no-nonsense mother. She would often upbraid Kim for her interest in astrology and fortune-telling, fiercely maintaining that everything which happened in the world could be explained by science. She supposed that deep down she believed her.

For Jean-Pierre, however, these forces were very real, and he treated them with the utmost respect. Suddenly Kim felt very small indeed, as though she was a new-born baby trying to understand the finer principles of nuclear physics.

The words "obeah" and "the walkers" kept returning to her mind. She was sure she had heard them somewhere before. She went into her father's study to look them up in the encyclopaedia there, but the Britannica was of little help.

She wished her Japanese father were here now. After all, he was a bestselling author and he knew all sorts of things that you couldn't normally find in books. However, he was off on a speaking tour of North America, and her English mother was out helping one of her old schoolfriends with some charity work, which Kim knew really meant that she was spending the night with her latest boyfriend. She was alone in the house.

It was nearly midnight. The only sound to be

28

heard was the tick-tick-tocking of the old grand-
father clock in the corner of the room. It had a
strangely soporific effect.

Brrrrriiiing!

The sudden noise made Kim almost jump out
of her skin. She reached over for the telephone
and picked it up before it had time to ring a second
time. Who could be calling her so late?

"Hello?"

"Hello, is that you, Kim? This is Mrs Tremayne,
you know, Claire's mother . . ."

"Oh, er, hi, Mrs Tremayne." Kim frowned. Claire
was one of the girls on her English Literature
course, but what was her mother doing ringing
Kim up at this late hour?

"I was just wondering if Claire was with you,"
said Mrs Tremayne. Even over the telephone Kim
could still hear that the woman was very worried
indeed. "She said she was meeting some friends
tonight and she hasn't returned home yet. I just
thought she might have turned up at your
place . . ."

"No, she hasn't, Mrs Tremayne," Kim said, and
added, "But I wouldn't worry—she's probably just
lost track of the time, that's all. I'm sure she'll be
home soon."

"Yes, well, I suppose you're right . . . I'm sorry
to have disturbed you . . . Goodnight, my dear."

"G'night." Kim put the phone down and shook
her head.

Really, Claire Tremayne was the limit! she
decided. She had a pretty good idea where Claire
would be now, but Kim thought that she could at

the very least have let her mother know that she'd be staying out late. But then Claire had the reputation of being thoughtless, and heartless, going out with whichever boy took her fancy that particular week, and to hell with the consequences. More than once Kim had told her that she'd regret her actions one day.

Kim stood up and yawned, just as the clock struck midnight. It was no time to worry about who Claire Tremayne was seeing tonight, she decided; now it was time to go to bed. She started to make her way to the stairs when she heard a peculiar noise, like a scratching or a soft tapping sound.

Kim looked around. Surely it couldn't be mice? The sound seemed to be coming from the front porch. Slowly she walked over to the front door. As she switched on the hallway light the noise stopped. She opened the front door and stepped out onto the porch.

"Hello, is there anybody there?" she called out.

There was no reply, and the driveway leading up to the front door was empty. There was a strange smell in the air, and she tried to place it.

It was like food which had gone off, the rank and rancid stink of decaying flesh . . .

She reached out behind her for the door knob. It was sticky and wet. She pulled her hand away and found, to her horror, that it was covered with blood. She turned around: the whole of the front door had been daubed with red, sticky blood.

Kim stepped back in disgust and her foot touched something on the stone step. She spun around, retching as she suddenly realised where the awful smell was coming from.

The carcass of a cockerel had been left on the doorstep, its stomach slit open and its bloody guts strewn all across the step. Its eyes had been gouged out of its head and its beak torn brutally from its head. The cock had obviously been dead for some days, and inside its gaping stomach foul-smelling maggots wriggled and crawled about.

Kim threw up there and then, and staggered back into the house, slamming the door shut behind her.

Claire Tremayne made her way through the undergrowth and sulked. She'd already ripped her best pair of designer jeans coming to this out-of-the-way place, and her hair looked as if she'd been dragged through several hedges backwards.

She yelped as she walked straight into the low-lying branch of a tree. Her Gucci shoes squelched and stuck in the mud from the day's rain.

This had better be worth it! she growled to herself, as she heaved her foot out of the quagmire.

Suddenly a cloud passed across the face of the moon, and Claire stood still. She certainly wasn't going to make another move until it reappeared; without the light of the moon she would most probably trip over and fall flat on her face. And there was no way that Claire Tremayne was going to get mud and filth all over her brand-new one-and-a-half-grand leather jacket!

Claire froze. She could just hear the harsh breathing of someone else.

For a second she realised what a fool she had been to come out here alone on this dark October night. Then she fingered the portable alarm in the side pocket of her leather jacket. If anyone tried to attack her now the shrieks of her alarm would be heard all the way down to the Thames! She might be a fool but she wasn't that big a fool!

The breathing was behind her now, and very, very close. She could have turned around to see who the other person was but for some reason she didn't dare. And for that very same reason she didn't dare run away either.

"Who's there?" she asked nervously.

"It's only me."

The voice was a whisper, barely audible above the wind rustling in the trees.

She felt the owner of the voice come up behind her.

"Is it really you?" she breathed, still not turning around.

"Of course, sweetheart. Who else could it be?"

Claire felt her hair being caressed, lovingly, by a hand. The touch felt curiously cold and clammy, and a shiver of terrible delight coursed through her body.

"But I don't understand . . ." she said.

"Hush, hush, sweetheart," the whisper said. "I was asleep, that's all. And now I'm awake . . . wide, wide awake . . . I missed you, you know. Did you miss me?"

Claire nodded. Scalding tears were pouring down her cheeks now.

"Good." There was a peculiar note of triumph

in the voice. "I'm glad . . . Turn around, sweet-heart, look at me . . ."

Claire nodded, but was unable to move. She found herself being grabbed by two cold and clammy hands.

"Look at me!"

Claire was spun around, and the two hands reached for her throat, pressing hard, sharp fingernails into the soft flesh, piercing the skin of her neck, rupturing her jugular vein. Her blood poured out in a fountain of scarlet.

"G'night, sweetheart," said the voice as Claire slumped to the ground and fell splashing into the mud, ruining her brand-new designer jacket that had cost her dad a cool one and a half thousand pounds.

Chapter 3

Mr Chippenham, the assistant chemistry teacher, shook his head sadly as he scanned his eyes over Jean-Pierre's essay. That was the trouble with Castlemare, he reflected; anyone whose parents had enough money could send their kids there, regardless of their ability. He remembered his own schooldays: then he'd had to study day and night just to make the grade and go to grammar school and then to university. These Castlemare kids, he reflected bitterly, they didn't know they were born.

"I'm afraid this simply isn't good enough, Jean-Pierre," he told the Haitian boy who was standing in front of his desk. "Another C-minus isn't going to help you pass your A-level chemistry next year now, is it?"

Jean-Pierre hung his head. "No, sir."

Mr Chippenham handed the paper back to Jean-Pierre and twirled his extravagant white moustache thoughtfully. "You've been at Castlemare for just over a week now, Jean-Pierre," he reminded him. "It must have been quite a wrench leaving your island in the Caribbean. You are happy here, aren't you?"

"Of course, sir," Jean-Pierre replied, and added politely, "But thank you for asking."

"A little more application, Jean-Pierre, that's what's needed," Mr Chippenham advised. "I know you've got it in you to get better grades. You can go and sit down now."

"Yes, sir. And thank you, sir."

Jean-Pierre walked slowly back to the work bench he shared with Calvin. As he sat down Calvin slapped him sympathetically on the back.

"Hard luck, Jean-Pierre," he said. "You got a rocket, eh?"

"What more does he want?" Jean-Pierre asked bitterly. "What has he got against me? I work as hard as I can already."

"You're telling me," said Calvin. "You've hardly been out of that library since you got here."

Calvin certainly wasn't complaining: with Jean-Pierre out of circulation, it meant that he had more opportunity to impress the more attractive female students at Castlemare.

"I work and I work yet I still don't seem to make the grade," Jean-Pierre complained. "While Francesca gets straight As with the minimum of effort."

"Hell, her mum's a Nobel Prize-winning chemist," said Calvin. "She probably helps her with her homework. Maybe you should try a spot of the old voodoo on old Chippenham there," Calvin suggested, and, before Jean-Pierre could protest, said: "OK, I'm sorry! Joke, OK?"

Jean-Pierre smiled. "OK, joke . . ."

"That's the way!" smiled Calvin as the bell rang

for the end of afternoon classes. "Lighten up a bit, Jean-Pierre!"

They left the science lab and made their way through the throngs of homeward-bound students to the car park. As they did, they bumped into Kim. She was dressed in a smart black suit from Comme des Garçons, which made a stark contrast to the wild grungy outfits she usually wore.

"Hi, Kim," Calvin said cheerfully, "I haven't seen you all day." He noticed her sombre outfit. "Who's died then?" he asked fliply.

"Sophie Ashford," came the curt reply.

"Whoops—me and my big mouth again," said Calvin, and apologised. "It was the funeral today, huh?"

"That's right," she said. "Her parents were really cut up about it. First Jeff, and now Sophie."

"Jeff Rawlinson?" asked Calvin, and then remembered. "He and Sophie used to go out with each other, right?"

Kim nodded. "Her parents looked on him as their own son," she said.

They walked slowly to Calvin's car, and then Kim turned to Jean-Pierre. She seemed to be debating whether to ask him something.

"Jean-Pierre, this might sound silly, but what do you know about chickens?"

"Chickens? What are you talking about?"

"On Tuesday night I found a dead cockerel on my doorstep," she said. "It had been sliced open and its guts spilt all over the step."

"Kim, you didn't tell me about this . . ." Calvin

was genuinely shocked. Even Jean-Pierre's dark face had paled.

"I didn't think it was important at the time," Kim continued. "I thought it was just some kids having a laugh and causing trouble. You know what they're like round here."

Calvin nodded. "Pretty much like us, I guess. So if you didn't think it was that important why are you mentioning it now?"

"Something Sophie's mother told me after the funeral." Kim's voice was trembling now. "It seems that just before she and Mr Ashford went off on their business trip to the States, leaving Sophie alone in the house—"

"Yes?"

"A gutted chicken was left on their front doorstep as well."

"Oh my God . . ."

"You must forget this, Kim," said Jean-Pierre, and his voice was trembling almost as much as hers. "It's just a coincidence. Some louts are causing trouble around here. How do you say? Having a lark? *Oui, c'est bien ça!*, Yes, that must be it!"

Calvin frowned; he had never seen Jean-Pierre act like this before. It was almost as if he were scared for his life.

"What's wrong, my man?" he asked. "Something's freaking you out, I can tell."

"N-nothing, nothing at all."

Kim was obviously still upset but now she was intrigued as well.

"Jean-Pierre, when I told you that Sophie was

going to be cremated you said you were pleased
for her—"

Jean-Pierre turned away, determined not to look
Kim in the face.

"You mentioned something about 'obeah' and
'the walkers'," she continued, determined to
pursue her point. "Who are they, Jean-Pierre?"

Jean-Pierre started to walk quickly away to
where his own car was parked.

"It's nothing, Kim," he lied and attempted to
affect an air of cheerfulness. "Just a silly superstition, nothing to worry about. It's just a joke,
that's all, a joke that's got out of hand . . ."

And with that, a very worried Jean-Pierre got
into his car and drove away, screeching out through
the open gates of Castlemare. Calvin and Kim
watched him go.

"Well, what do you make of that?" asked Calvin.

"He was scared out of his wits," remarked Kim.

Calvin put an arm over her shoulder. "But how
about you, sweetheart?" he asked, genuinely concerned. "How are you feeling?"

Kim smiled. "You might all think I'm a dizzy
would-be witch who takes more notice of her hor-
oscope than what's going on around her," she said
cheerfully, "but it's gonna take more than a chop-
ped-up chicken to faze me!"

Calvin hugged her tightly to him. "That's my
girl!" he said encouragingly.

"You know something, Calvin Charles," Kim said
seriously, "when you're not on the make and trying
to prove your macho credentials by picking up

anything that's got a pulse and is wearing a skirt, then you can actually be quite a good friend!"

"Thanks, Kim," he said gratefully. "But keep it to yourself, OK? Think what it would do to my reputation!"

"OK, I promise," she said. "Are you going on down for some sushi at Tokyo Joe's tonight?"

Calvin shook his head. "No cold raw fish for me," he said. "Mister Chippenham said I could stay late in the lab tonight, for some last-minute revision."

"It's probably only so you can lock up for him while he gets himself off his face in the pub," Kim sniggered. Among the teaching staff at Castlemare Chippenham was a notorious boozer; it constantly amazed his fellow members of staff that he had managed to hold on to his job at the school for so long.

"Who cares?" said Calvin. "I need the extra study-time. Remember, unlike you arty English Lit students, we Chemistry guys live in the real world and we've got mid-term exams next week!"

"I know—just before Hallowe'en too."

Calvin flung down his pencil, and looked at his Swatch. It was a quarter to midnight. He'd been studying for over four hours now, and if he saw as much as one more chemical formula tonight he swore he'd go out of his mind.

He looked across the chemistry lab at Francesca; as usual she looked like a million dollars. No one would have known that she'd been studying for as long as he had.

She looked up at him and smiled. "Are you calling it a day?" she asked.

He nodded. "We're the last two here," he said, and yawned. "You want a lift home?"

"Thanks," she said.

A girl shouldn't walk home alone at night," he said approvingly. "There are a lot of crazies out there."

"There's still been no word from Claire Tremayne then?"

Calvin shook his head. "Her mum's worried sick. No one knows where she's gone or what's happened to her."

"If I know Claire it'll have something to do with a boy," Francesca said, and indicated the textbook in front of her. "I've just got to finish this chapter Calvin, and then I'll be ready."

"OK, sweetheart." Calvin stood up and stretched. "I'm just going to collect my jacket from the locker room, OK?"

"OK," she said, without raising her eyes from her book, "see you in five minutes then . . ."

Calvin left the chemistry lab and walked down the long empty corridor leading to the lockers. He liked Castlemare at this time of night, and there had been more than one occasion when he'd stayed behind after school with one of his fellow students for some late-night "revision".

The fact that most of those fellow students had been extremely sexy sixth-form girls had had absolutely nothing to do with it, of course; nor had the fact that very little revision had actually got done on those nights. Well, at least not the kind that mouldy old Mr Chippenham would grade him on, anyway.

Not that he felt that way towards Francesca, of course. Sure, she was nothing less than drop-dead gorgeous, but she and Calvin had known each other since they were kids, as their parents were old friends, and he treated her more as a sister or a good pal than anything else.

In fact, he preferred to treat most of the girls at Castlemare like buddies rather than potential girlfriends. He knew he had this reputation for being a bit of a ladykiller, but then that had all been down to Jeff Rawlinson.

Pretty-boy Jeff, who always got all the girls, had delighted in making Calvin feel inferior; so when Jeff had gone, Calvin had seen his opportunity and taken on the mantle of prize hunk, chief ladykiller and general good-time guy at Castlemare. It felt good, not to be walking in Jeff's shadow for a change; and though Calvin knew it was wrong there was still a part of him that was secretly pleased Jeff was dead.

Calvin's footsteps echoed on the parquet floor down the long corridors of Castlemare. This wing of the school building was the spookiest, he decided; it was part of the old country mansion around which Castlemare had been built, and at nights you could almost imagine the ghosts of all those who had lived and died here down through the centuries as they floated along the empty wood-panelled corridors.

Some people said that Castlemare was riddled with secret passages, and there were even those who believed the school was built on the site of an old pagan burial ground. Late at night, with the autumn moon shimmering in through the long high windows and the wind whistling eerily through the yew trees in the courtyard, Calvin would have believed anything.

Crash!

Calvin froze. Was it his imagination or had he heard something?

"Frannie? Is that you?" he called out.

There was no reply, just the sound of his own voice as it echoed and re-echoed down the cold and empty corridors.

Calvin shivered and then giggled nervously to himself.

Don't be such a dweeb! he silently reproved himself. *This is Castlemare High. It is not—are you listening to me, Calvin, my man?—I repeat, it is not a haunted house from a second-rate late-night horror movie!*

Nevertheless, as he walked down the corridor he kept darting a worried look behind him. But there was nothing to see, only his shadow, grotesquely magnified by the moonlight through the windows.

Calvin finally reached the locker room, and found his leather jacket. He looked warily about him; he still couldn't shake off this feeling that he was being watched.

He made his way back along the corridors to the chemistry lab, now whistling nervously to himself. Outside, the wind blew branches of the yew trees against the window-panes, and the moonlight illuminated the dusty old portraits of the school's founders which lined the walls.

Calvin stopped to look at one of them, a particularly severe-looking old man who had been the headmaster at the turn of the century when Castlemare had still been a boys-only public school. *Doctor Heironymous Grimshanks*. The name suited him well, Calvin decided. He looked just like an extra from a bad episode of *The Munsters* TV series. He pulled a face at him.

And then he froze again.

Click. Click.

There was no mistaking it this time. Someone was following him!

Click. Click. Click.

Whoever it might be was walking on tip toes, and Calvin could just hear the tip-tip-tapping of their steel-tipped boots as they trod on the finely polished floor.

Click. Click. Click. Click.

They were almost upon him now. Calvin felt the hairs on the back of his neck rise and his heart pounded madly in his chest.

He clenched his fists and took a deep breath.

Well, buster, if it's a fight you want . . .

He spun around, fists raised, ready to throw himself upon his attacker.

Miaow?

Calvin gasped a sigh of relief and laughed. He bent down and picked up the large tabby cat, nuzzling it affectionately.

"Demosthenes, you mangy old moggy!" Calvin chided the caretaker's cat. "You don't know the fright you gave me! Has Mr Bream sent you out in search of mice again?"

Demosthenes purred in a superior manner, as if to indicate that he thought Calvin was a very stupid human being indeed.

Calvin continued to stroke the cat, and hugged its furry body to him. The cat's presence was strangely comforting as he looked out of the window at the dark and threatening clouds which were passing over the moon.

Hey, look at me! Calvin reproved himself. *A week to go until Hallowe'en and I'm letting myself get as spooked as Kim! Loosen up, bud!*

Suddenly he felt Demosthenes tense in his arms, and his back arch. The cat hissed.

"Demosthenes? What's up?"

The cat sprang out of Calvin's arms and pelted back down the corridor as fast as his legs would carry him. Calvin watched the cat disappear and then turned and peered ahead into the half-light at the end of the corridor where it turned off to the right and led to the science wing.

Was it just a trick of the moonlight or was there something moving there in the shadows?

He heard the leaves of the yew trees rustling outside.

Or was it something else?

"Sweetheart . . . sweetheart . . . where are you, sweetheart?"

Calvin stalked forward, scarcely daring to breathe. His fists clenched once more, but this time in dread anticipation.

Bong!

Calvin spun round, but the sound was coming from one of the old-fashioned clocks which lined the walls of Castlemare and which were tolling midnight. It was hanging from the wall at a peculiar angle, and he reached up to adjust it—and a powerful arm grabbed him from behind, dragging him crashing to the floor.

Calvin rolled over and stared at the figure towering over him, terrifyingly silhouetted against the full moon. He saw the blue baseball jacket, dirtied and torn, and the designer jeans, spattered with mud. He recognised with horror the powerful gym-trained body, and the dark hair, now dripping wet and dishevelled.

Calvin turned his face away in disgust when he saw that *things* were crawling and wriggling in that hair now—worms and maggots, insects and spiders, all the night-time creatures of the graveyard.

He forced himself to look again at his attacker. And then saw the eyes. There were no pupils—just two hideous, mocking slits of white.

"It can't be you!" Calvin gasped as he scrambled away from his attacker and tried to drag himself to his feet.

"Oh yes it can be!" the creature hissed, and approached Calvin. Its hands were outstretched, and, even in his horror, Calvin saw that the finger-nails were filthy and bloody.

The creature reached for Calvin's neck and squeezed. Calvin reached up, trying to break free of its grip, but the creature was much too strong.

45

Its strength was more than human, almost the strength of a blood-maddened wild dog.

Globs of slime dripped from its mouth, falling onto Calvin's face, and the creature increased the pressure on Calvin's throat. He slammed Calvin against the wall, and bashed his head against the wood panels. Again and again and again.

The last thing Calvin heard was the creature's maniacal cackle as it repeated over and over: "I'm dead! You're dead! I'm dead! And now you're dead! We're all dead!"

"Calvin, are you all right?"

Calvin came to, and found Francesca bending over him in concern. He shot bolt upright and looked around nervously. The corridor was empty.

"Jeff!" he cried. "It was Jeff Rawlinson! He was here!"

Francesca shook her head. "Jeff's dead, Calvin, you know that."

"He was here—he tried to kill me."

"You've had a bad dream, that's all," Francesca said softly. "When you hadn't come back after twenty minutes I came looking for you. I found you here in the corridor, out cold. You must have had a nasty bump on the head."

Calvin suddenly found he had a raging headache. He rubbed the back of his head: already there was a painful swelling there.

Francesca nodded over to the old-fashioned clock which lay on the floor next to them. Its face was smashed.

"That must have fallen off the wall and hit you on the head," she said.

Calvin nodded. "I remember reaching up to fix it," he said slowly, and then shook his head. "No, it was Jeff. I tell you, Frannie, it was Jeff!"

Francesca sighed. "Jeff is dead," she repeated firmly. "He's buried out there in Highgate Cemetery. Are you seriously trying to tell me that he's risen from his grave? That's impossible and you know it!"

"I know, I know." Calvin didn't know what to think anymore. "People can't rise from the dead. But, Frannie, it was so real . . ."

"But it was just a nightmare."

Calvin frowned. "Yeah, I suppose you're right," he said, and then looked at the left sleeve of his leather jacket. He reacted instinctively and violently brushed something off it to the ground.

"What are you doing?" asked Francesca.

"Do you still think I was dreaming?" Calvin asked heavily. He pointed down to the floor, to the thing he had swiped from his jacket.

It was a maggot.

Chapter 4

"I feel awful," said Murphy, propped up in bed, her face a distinct shade of green. It was nine o'clock at night and she had been in bed for the whole of Saturday.

"You look it," Kim agreed.

"Thank you very much."

"That's what comes from eating raw fish at home instead of coming out with us last night for *designer* raw fish!" Kim said.

"You mean sushi."

"That's right," said Kim. "If it's not absolutely fresh, fish can carry all sorts of nasty germs."

"I think I'm going to die," Murphy decided miserably.

Kim chuckled. "You'll survive. It's only a mild case of food poisoning. If you want I'll cast you a get-well spell!"

"Now that would really finish me off," Murphy laughed.

Kim looked at her watch. "I have to be going now," she announced. "I said I'd meet Calvin at nine-thirty."

"Oh yes?" Murphy asked suggestively, sensing

the possibility of a little bit of gossip. "A romantic evening encounter by any chance?"

"Hardly," the Japanese girl groaned, and then shivered. "Calvin and I are going corpse-hunting!"

After Kim had left, Murphy turned over and tried to fall asleep. After half an hour, she gave up and got out of bed. She threw on a dressing-gown, and, on distinctly wobbly legs, made her way downstairs to make herself a night-time drink. Since it was a Saturday night her parents were out and she was alone in the big empty house.

As she stirred her mug of hot chocolate, she thought she could hear something.

Tap. Tap. Tap.

She shrugged. It was probably just the wind, brushing the branches of a tree against the kitchen window, she decided. It was certainly nothing to get worried about.

She moved into the living-room and settled herself down in front of the TV. She zapped the set on and curled up on the sofa as the Saturday-night movie came on.

"Sweetheart . . . sweetheart . . ."

Murphy muted the TV and stood up. She put her mug down on the coffee table and walked into the kitchen.

"Sweetheart . . . sweetheart . . ."

There was no one about, and Murphy began to get worried. Was she really hearing someone call out to her? Or was she imagining things?

There was a hissing from the corner of the kitchen, and Murphy burst out laughing. The kitchen radiator was playing up again, she realised. Her dad had been promising to get it fixed for months now, but as usual nothing had been done.

The hissing of the air in the empty pipes probably did sound like someone whispering, especially when her head was befuddled with illness.

She turned to go back to the living-room, when—

"Sweetheart . . . sweetheart . . ."

There was no doubt about it this time, Murphy concluded.

This was no dodgy radiator her father hadn't got round to fixing: this was a real live scuzzball! It was almost Hallowe'en, she remembered: it could even be some kids pushing their luck with spot of early Trick or Treat.

Well, if you're out to scare people, whoever you are, then you've gone and picked the wrong house! Murphy thought determinedly.

She strode up to the kitchen door as a car screeched to a halt outside in the driveway of her next door neighbour. Murphy pulled open the door.

"OK, who is it?" she demanded.

There was no reply. The branches of the tree tapped gently against the kitchen window. The back driveway to Murphy's house was empty save for a startled owl which, on seeing her, flew away.

Murphy scolded herself for being so jumpy. From across the garden fence her nextdoor neighbour Mrs Armitage waved a cheery hello as she carried her day's shopping from the back of her car.

Had Mrs Armitage frightened whoever it was away? Murphy asked herself. Or was she letting her imagination get the better of her again?

"Hello there, dear!" Mrs Armitage cooed over the garden fence. "I hear you're not feeling too well."

"It's nothing, just something I ate . . ."

"Well, hurry along indoors, my dear," the forty-something woman urged. "You'll catch your death on the doorstep in your nightgown! The weather forecast says there's going to be a storm later tonight."

"Sure, Mrs Armitage!" Murphy grinned at her neighbour's fussing, and turned to go inside. Then she paused, and called out, "You haven't seen anyone hanging around outside have you, Mrs Armitage?"

"Why, no, dear," came the reply. "Is there anything wrong?"

Murphy shook her head. "No, nothing at all, I must have been imagining it, that's all," she said.

Mrs Armitage's voice was suddenly full of concern. "If you're worried about anything, dear, I can send Peter around," she said. "I'm sure he'd love to keep you company . . ."

"No, please no!" Murphy said, a little too emphatically to be polite. Mrs Armitage's son Peter was a nice boy, but, if Murphy had to choose someone to keep her company and provide her with interesting conversation, she'd probably be better off with one of the fish from Francesca's father's aquarium!

Murphy waved goodbye to Mrs Armitage and then noticed something on the kitchen doorstep.

She knelt down to take a closer look, and quickly stood up again when she saw what it was.

Murphy pulled a face and shivered. She knew that it was foolish and that they weren't in any way harmful, but they had always revolted her, ever since she had been a little girl and had sneaked a look into her dad's fishing bag, upsetting a whole tub of them.

She hated maggots.

"Calvin, I'm not sure that this is such a good idea after all."

"Of course it is," said Calvin. "It's *my* idea, isn't it?"

"That's what's worrying me."

Calvin chuckled and reached out his arms to Kim who was sitting at the top of the high brick wall they had both just scaled. "Now let me help you down."

Kim let herself be lifted down to the muddy ground, narrowly missing scratching herself on the nettles which grew along the perimeter wall.

"Breaking into Highgate Cemetery at night is also illegal," she pointed out.

"That's OK," he said, and picked up the back-pack which he had thrown over the wall first of all. "Remember: Dad works at the American Embassy. If we get caught then I've got diplomatic immunity!"

"But I haven't!"

"Hey, chill out. We'll think of something!"

Calvin turned to look around at the cemetery. In the moonlight and the heavy rain it looked even spookier and more desolate than it had done when they'd all gone there on a school outing earlier in the term.

There were gravestones as far as they could see, some almost completely covered by the ivy which had been left to grow over the years as the people buried there had slowly become forgotten by their loved ones. Mock-Gothic crypts, belonging to wealthy familes, were dotted around together with ornate sepulchres and solid-looking mausoleums.

In the undergrowth little nocturnal animals skittered and crawled, all seeking refuge from the pouring rain which was turning the already uneven and treacherous ground into a quagmire.

"Lovely," Kim said sarcastically. "To think I could be at home right now in front of a warm fire, watching a nice video nasty. Why did I ever let you talk me into this?"

"Because you want to know what's happened to Jeff Rawlinson just as much as I do," said Calvin, suddenly serious. "Because you're the only person at Castlemare who even half-believes that he might have risen from the dead."

Kim touched his arm. "Calvin, you did receive a big knock on the head last night . . ."

"So?" He rubbed the lump on the back of his head; it was still hurting.

"So maybe you did imagine it all, just like Francesca said."

"Then if we find his dead body I'll shut up, OK?" he said angrily. "And don't you want to know who's been desecrating all those graves? Don't you want to meet one of those vampires you're always talking about?"

Kim shuddered. "Quite frankly, no." She turned around haughtily and made as if to leave.

"Look, sweetheart, I'm sorry I snapped at you, OK?" Calvin said and took her hand. "Now follow me; one false move around here and you're going to fall headlong into somebody's grave!"

Grumbling, Kim allowed herself to be led through the twisting lanes of the cemetery, slipping in the mud and more than once stumbling over tombstones which had subsided into the wet and soft ground, or tripping over the long snaking roots of trees.

They trudged slowly up a small hillock as the rain continued to pour down, plastering Kim's black hair to her face, and soaking through her leather jacket and the several layers of pullovers she was wearing underneath.

Calvin, on the other hand, didn't seem to notice the rain, even though he was becoming just as drenched as Kim. He moved forward with a steely determination, ignoring the branches which were being lashed brutally into his face by the wind, which was rising, and the mud which sloshed about his feet, seeping into his expensive Italian boots.

He must be really worried, thought Kim, and then realised what was really driving Calvin.

He wants to make sure that Jeff really is dead,

she decided, and recalled the time when Jeff had been alive.

Then it had been Jeff who had always got the sexiest and most sought-after girl, Jeff who had always got straight As in all his exams, Jeff who had always been the teacher's pet, and Jeff who had always been the life and soul of every single party he turned up to.

Calvin, attractive, intelligent, popular—but not *quite* as attractive, intelligent and popular as Jeff—had always been envious of Jeff. It was a jealousy which had obsessed him, and, when Jeff had unexpectedly died, Calvin had at last had the opportunity to step outside his rival's shadow.

Kim shuddered involuntarily, and prayed that Jeff really was dead. If not, she couldn't be certain that Calvin wouldn't try to kill him there and then.

"Here we are," he said.

They had stopped in front of an old granite mausoleum at the top of the hillock. The mausoleum was set in a grove of yew trees, whose sinuous roots seemed to encircle it protectively.

Diabolical-looking stone gargoyles glared out from the walls of the mausoleum, while presiding over the arched door which led into the tomb's interior there was carved the figure of an angel. Kim noted wryly that one of its wings was missing: the vandals who had desecrated other graves in the cemetery had obviously been here as well. They'd left the gargoyles alone though, she noticed.

"Here we are where?" she asked.

Through the driving rain Calvin pointed out the

legend above the doorway. There, carved in Gothic letters, was a name: RAWLINSON.

"It's Jeff's family crypt," he explained. "Now we'll know for certain if he's dead or not."

"You mean we're going to go in there?" Kim asked in horror.

"That's right," said Calvin, as though it was the most normal thing in the world to attempt to break into someone's tomb on a rainy Saturday night. "If Jeff's buried in there, then I'll know that I imagined what I saw last night. And if he's not . . ."

"Calvin, I don't like it."

"What are you scared of?" he asked, and then laughed. "Ghosts? The walking dead?"

"Don't be silly," she snapped, as that was exactly what she was scared of. She pointed to the door of the crypt; it was made of iron and it was firmly closed. "Anyway, nothing and no one could get into or out of this place!"

"It could have been locked from the inside," Calvin said, and opened his backpack. He took out a metal crowbar and began to prise open the door like a man possessed.

"No, Calvin, no!" cried Kim, and frantically began to try to stop him.

"I have to see if he's dead or not, don't you understand!" he cried, and shook himself free of her. "I have to know one way or the other! I have to be sure!"

As he pushed her away, she slipped in the mud and fell over. In panic, she blindly reached out to snatch hold of something, anything, to stop her sliding any further down the hillock.

Calvin threw down his crowbar and bent down to help her up.

"Kim, I'm sorry, sweetheart!" he said. "Are you all right?"

Kim gasped, and attempted to pick herself up. "I'm fine," she said, and looked down at her Lycra leggings; they were covered in mud. "I managed to grab hold of a tree root or something."

Calvin stared down, wild-eyed, at the object which Kim had grabbed to break her fall. Kim saw the look of horror in the young American's eyes and made herself look as well.

She was not holding the root of a tree.

She was holding a human hand.

Cold, black and stiff, but still recognisably a human hand.

A female hand.

"Oh, my God . . ."

The heavy rains had washed away the earth to reveal the corpse which had been buried just a few inches below the surface. Kim turned away, but Calvin had to know what had been hidden there. He scrabbled away at the wet and crumbling earth with his bare hands; and suddenly he felt the bile rise in his throat.

There, staring malevolently back at him through the wild and torrential rain, was the bloated face of Claire Tremayne. Her once pretty features were now set in a maniacal and perverted grin.

Her throat had been cut—no, not cut, *gouged* open—and from out of her open wounds, writhing and wriggling amidst the long-congealed blood, gorging themselves on her dead flesh, were hundreds upon hundreds of maggots.

Chapter 5

"So what were you two kids doing in the cemetery anyway?" Police Sergeant Evans asked gruffly.

It was two o'clock in the morning and he should have been at home in bed with his wife; the only times he ever seemed to get called out at this time of the night were when one of those bloody rich kids at Castlemare had got themselves in a bit of trouble.

Too rich for their own good! he thought.

Calvin looked up from the table in the police station where he had been nursing a mug of coffee for the past half-hour or so. His face was ashen, and his eyes were rimmed with red.

"I told you," he said. "We wanted some time on our own . . ." He glanced over at Kim, who was looking just as pale and worried as he was. She didn't say a word, and he was grateful to her for not contradicting his lie.

"So you just did a bunk over the cemetery walls in the middle of a downpour?" Sergeant Evans didn't sound particularly convinced.

"That's right," said Kim. "And when it started to

rain even more heavily we decided to shelter by one of those tombs. That's when we found . . ."

She lowered her eyes as the horrible memory of Claire's ravaged and half-eaten face returned to her mind. She began to sob uncontrollably and Calvin took her in his arms.

"Yes, well, perhaps it's just as well you did . . ." harrumphed Evans who had never been that much of an expert when it came to dealing with weeping females. "If you two kids hadn't discovered her when you did she might have been lying there for months. At least after only a week out there she hadn't decomposed too badly. At least we can still identify her."

"Can we go now?" asked Calvin.

Evans didn't answer his question. Instead he shook his head despairingly.

"What is it about you kids from Castlemare?" he asked rhetorically, and there was more than a touch of resentment in his voice. "You have all the money you could ever hope for, the best of everything, an upbringing and an education my little 'uns would give their right arms for. And yet you keep on flouting the law as if it was only meant for other people and not for your privileged lot."

"We didn't kill her!" Calvin exploded and slammed his fist angrily down on the table.

"I didn't say you did, sonny," said Evans. "And hopefully we'll find the person responsible. But there is the little matter of your breaking into the cemetery at night . . ."

"If we hadn't done we wouldn't have found Claire," Kim pointed out. "I mean, her body . . ."

"You can't charge us," Calvin said. "My father's a diplomat—I've got diplomatic immunity."

Evans wasn't impressed. "The young lady hasn't, Mr Charles," he said, making the same point Kim had made earlier. "And, diplomatic immunity or not, I can still have you deported from this country if I choose to. Your father would probably lose his job as well."

Calvin fell silent. He hadn't considered that possibility; once again he hadn't thought his actions through. Evans was in control now, and he was enjoying it enormously.

"But, as you say, Ms Nishida, if you hadn't climbed the walls of the cemetery then we wouldn't have found the corpse."

"So what exactly are you saying—Sergeant" asked Calvin.

"This might not be the first time you two have broken into the cemetery," Evans said. "Last night several more gravestones were desecrated... Where were you two last night?"

"We were at Tokyo Joe's till eleven!" protested Kim, then added: "Well, at least I was ..."

"And you, Mr Charles, can anyone vouch for where you were last night?"

Calvin didn't know what to say. If he said that he had been with Francesca until midnight then the whole story of Jeff Rawlinson would come out into the open. And then Evans would know the real reason why they had both been in the cemetery: he didn't want to be branded as a graverobber for the rest of his life.

"I repeat, Mr Charles, can anyone vouch for your whereabouts last night?"

"Yes, Sergeant," came a familiar voice from the doorway, and Evans, Calvin and Kim turned around. "I can vouch for Calvin."

"*Jean-Pierre?*"

Evans' face coloured; he'd already met Jean-Pierre when the boy's father had come around to the police station when the alarm on his new house had been installed. Unlike the other kids at Castlemare Jean-Pierre had always struck him as a decent law-abiding sort. What was more, Jean-Pierre's father had given him and his wife tickets for his embassy's swanky Christmas do. A nice family, were the Denfers, Evans had decided.

"Calvin was with me for most of the evening, and then we met up with the others when they left Tokyo Joe's," Jean-Pierre said. "We went back to my house to listen to some music. They must have both left the house at about four-thirty this morning." He looked meaningfully at Calvin. "Isn't that right, Calvin?"

"Er, yeah . . . sure, that's right . . ."

"So you see, Sergeant Evans, Calvin and Kim couldn't possibly have had anything to do with the vandalism in the cemetery," Jean-Pierre concluded, and then craftily added, "Of course, if you don't believe me I can always ask my father to come around and make a statement to that effect . . ."

"That won't be necessary, Jean-Pierre," Evans blustered, and then turned to Calvin and Kim. "All right, you two, you can go now."

"It'll be a pleasure," Calvin muttered darkly, and

62

followed Jean-Pierre and Kim out of the police station.

When they were in the open air Calvin slapped Jean-Pierre on the back. "That was marvellous, my man! I owe you one."

Jena-Pierre acknowledged the thanks, but didn't return the smile. "I suspected he would be unwilling to call my bluff," he said.

"But how did you know we were there?" asked Kim.

Jean-Pierre hesitated for a moment and then said: "I was driving past when I saw Calvin's car parked in the station car park. I imagined he might be in trouble and came to help."

Kim regarded the Haitian boy suspiciously. It was obvious to her that he wasn't telling either of them the whole story.

"There's something else, Jean-Pierre, isn't there? Something else that's worrying you?"

Jean-Pierre looked into the cloudy night sky. "I know what you were doing in the cemetery," he said.

"But how?"

"Francesca told me about what happened last night," he replied. "I hope that she is right and that what you saw, Calvin, was merely a figment of your imagination."

"I didn't imagine it, Jean-Pierre," Calvin stated flatly. "I saw Jeff Rawlinson. He tried to strangle me, for crying out loud! Somewhere Jeff Rawlinson is still alive!"

"And then, for all our sakes, I pray to the great lord Damballah that he is indeed alive . . ."

Calvin and Kim looked curiously at their friend. "What are you talking about, Jean-Pierre?"

Jean-Pierre turned to them with a forced smile.

"It is late, and your car is over there, Calvin. I suggest that we all go home and sleep now. Things will surely be much brighter and clearer in the morning, *n'est-ce pas?*"

And with that Jean-Pierre ran through the rain to his car and drove away.

Calvin crossed to his own car and opened the door for Kim. "Can I drive you home?"

"Yeah . . . thanks . . ."

Kim walked slowly over, seemingly oblivious to the falling rain.

"Anything wrong, sweetheart?" Calvin asked.

"I'm still a little shaken up after finding Claire," she said. "And that name Jean-Pierre just used . . ."

"Dam-something or other?"

"Damballah," she said. "He used it once before, and it's been bothering me ever since. I thought I'd heard it somewhere, or read it in a book. And now I've finally remembered what it means."

"So what does it mean?"

Kim didn't answer; instead she continued to think aloud. "Jean-Pierre's a Christian, he told us. So are most of the population of Haiti. So why would he pray to Damballah now?"

"Look, just who is this Damballah guy anyway?" asked Calvin, growing a little irritated at Kim's mysteriousness.

"The Great Serpent," Kim said. "Calvin, Damballah is a voodoo god."

Chapter 6

"Murphy, I want you to have this."

Intrigued, Murphy gazed down at the object which Jean-Pierre was offering her.

She'd been pleasantly surprised when he had called round to her house that Sunday morning to see how she was feeling; after all, she and he weren't exactly the greatest of friends yet. She wondered what ulterior motive he might have in giving her this finely carved pendant.

For a second she thought that he might have been trying to flirt with her—and he was a very good-looking guy, Murphy had noticed. And it seemed quite odd—and incredibly good timing!— that he had called round just as her parents had left to go out for their customary Sunday lunch in their favourite restaurant.

Without thinking she pulled her duvet cover closer to her body: after all, it wasn't every day that you had one of the hunkiest-looking guys in the whole of Castlemare sitting by your bedside!

But then she sadly reconciled herself to the fact that no one as average-looking as she was would ever attract the attention of someone like Jean-Pierre. And besides that, she couldn't imagine the oh-so-serious and studious Jean-Pierre being interested in any girl at all, let alone her: well, at least not until his A-level studies were over.

"What is it, Jean-Pierre?" she asked, as she fingered the finely carved image of a serpent attached to a leather thong so long that she could loop it at least three times around her hands.

"Let us say it is a fetish."

Murphy cocked an eyebrow in interest. She'd read all about fetishes in some of the banned scandal rags that her fellow students used to pass underneath the schooldesks.

Jean-Pierre noticed her interested expression and laughed.

"Not the sort of fetish you think!" he said, and wagged his finger at her in a gesture of mock reproval. "A fetish is a sacred object filled with the power of a *loa* . . ."

"A what?" She wished Kim were here now; at least she might have some idea of what the Haitian was talking about.

Jean-Pierre tried to search for the right explanation. "A *loa* is—*comment se dit*?—let us say, it is a spirit, a guardian angel if you like . . ."

Murphy fingered the amulet curiously. It was a nice thought of Jean-Pierre's, she knew, but the amulet was still pretty ugly.

The coiled serpent stared back at her with its wide, hungry jaws open. So lifelike did it seem that she wouldn't have been at all surprised if, given half the chance, it suddenly sprang to life and ripped her apart with its sharp and deadly fangs.

"It will keep you safe in times of danger," Jean-Pierre said portentously.

"Like a lucky charm, you mean?" she asked, and then, to lighten the mood, added, "Like a rabbit's foot?"

Jean-Pierre smiled indulgently. "If you like."

"But why give it to me, Jean-Pierre?" she asked. "I mean, it's a sweet gift and all that, but . . ."

Jean-Pierre turned his face away. "As I said, it is a fetish to keep you safe in times of danger. Let us just say that it is a silly superstition on my part, *d'accord*?"

"I could have done with this two nights ago," she said. "When I came down with food-poisoning after eating that dodgy fish."

"Ah yes, the children of Agwé can carry all sorts of terrible things . . ."

Murphy frowned. At times Jean-Pierre could be so blasted inscrutable, she decided, even more so than Kim; and at least Kim had an excuse, at least she was half-Japanese! Jean-Pierre could make even the most casual comment seem laden with meaning!

"Things are getting out of hand now," he said mysteriously. "I fear for my friends . . ."

"What do you mean, Jean-Pierre, what's getting out of hand?"

He turned away from her, and stared out through her bedroom window. It was still the early afternoon, but already the October sky was dark and threatening with storm clouds.

"Castlemare is not like my home in Port-au-

67

Prince, the capital of Haiti," he said. "There we respected the dead and they respected us—"

"*What?*"

"Already terrible things have happened here, things which should not happen in England," Jean-Pierre continued. "Since I am arrived at this school a girl only my age has died of a heart attack; graves have been destroyed by vandals; and yet another girl, Claire Tremayne, has gone . . . missing."

When Jean-Pierre mentioned Claire's name there was a strange tremor in his voice; as *if he knows more than he's saying*, thought Murphy, but she didn't say anything.

"A dead cockerel has been left at the door of Kim," Jean-Pierre added. "And even you, Murphy: last night, I know that you were not left in peace—"

"I was just letting my imagination get the better of me," she protested. "The air in the pipes was whistling and I thought someone was calling my name. The trees outside were tapping against the window and it sounded like—"

Suddenly an eminently sensible thought struck her. "Wait a minute—how did you know what happened last night?"

Jena-Pierre couldn't seem to see why Murphy was so concerned. "Why, Peter Armitage, of course."

"Peter Armitage?" Murphy was confused.

"I was talking to him on the telephone this morning," Jean-Pierre said. "Didn't you speak to his mother last night and ask her if she had seen anyone lurking about?"

Murphy breathed a sigh—of relief? She wasn't

entirely sure. "Yes, that's right, I did speak to Mrs Armitage last night."

"Then that is how I know just how frightened you were last night," Jean-Pierre said simply. "How else could I know such a thing?" He chuckled. "I am not a magician, you know, Murphy!"

Murphy laughed: just like last night she was allowing her wild imagination to run away with her. She put it down to the Celt in her: her dad had always said that, when it came to making up stories out of nothing, there was no one to beat the Irish! She looked back down at the amulet Jean-Pierre had given to her.

"Promise me that you will wear it, Murphy," he urged her.

"I promise, Jean-Pierre."

"Then let me see you put it on now," he said.

Murphy shrugged and hung the heavy amulet around her neck. The leather thong on it stretched almost down to her waist. Jean-Pierre smiled.

"You need have nothing more to fear now," he said. "Damballah will protect you."

"Damballah?" Murphy repeated.

To the best of her knowledge, she had never heard the name spoken before, and yet the ponderous syllables of the unfamiliar word seemed oddly menacing.

"The great Lord of Voodoo," Jean-Pierre said, as matter-of-factly as if he had been talking about his Sunday afternoon shopping list, "the Serpent King. Do not fear, Murphy—with the mighty Snake on your side nothing can harm you!"

The room suddenly felt very cold. Outside the

storm clouds were gathering, and in the distance Murphy could hear the ominous roll of faraway thunder. She was suddenly very frightened indeed. She had only ever heard of one other "snake god" before; and she knew what had happened to Adam and Eve in the Garden of Eden.

"Jean-Pierre, I think you'd better go now," she said steadily.

Jean-Pierre began to protest—*a little too forcefully*? she asked herself and she added, "It's starting to rain."

"Ah, of course, you are tired and you want to be left alone," he said, as ever the perfect gentleman.

Murphy nodded and Jean-Pierre politely said his goodbyes and turned to go.

For a long time after he had left Murphy lay back on her pillow, wondering. What was Jean-Pierre so frightened about? Voodoo? That was just a stupid superstition, wasn't it? This was the twentieth century after all!

Who or what was Damballah really? And what did all of these unanswered questions have to do with her, and Kim, and the missing Claire, and poor, dead Sophie?

It was only after half an hour of tormenting herself with these thoughts that she realised that, for all this time, she had been clutching the image of the Serpent God to her breast as though her very life depended on it.

If she had got out of bed when Jean-Pierre had left she would have seen something else which would have worried her even more. Her bedroom was directly above the kitchen door, and if she had looked out of her bedroom window, she would have seen Jean-Pierre pause as he left the house by the back door.

He crouched down, and seemed to be examining something in the bushes by the kitchen doorstep. He glanced up nervously at Murphy's bedroom window, to check that she wasn't spying on him. And then he reached into the bush and pulled out the object that Murphy had missed when she had said goodnight to Mrs Armitage the previous evening.

It was the gutted carcass of a chicken. As he held it his hands, the filthy feasting maggots wriggled and oozed out of it, and slowly crawled up Jean-Pierre's outstretched arm.

"Are you sure you're gonna be OK?" Calvin asked the pretty Maria-Teresa as they sheltered under an umbrella outside the trendy art cinema in the main street running through Hampstead.

The dark-haired and well-dressed South American girl chuckled. "Why shouldn't I be?" she said. "I only live a short walk away on the edge of the Heath."

"It's a dark night, and it's raining," Calvin insisted. "I could give you a lift home if you want . . . ." He winked flirtatiously at her, making it obvious that what he had in mind was more than just a simple lift home.

"I'm going to be much safer walking on my own than in a car with you, Calvin Charles," she laughed. "The girls at Castlemare have told me all about you."

"Lies," Calvin laughed, "all lies!"

The truth was that Calvin had had his eye on the sexy daughter of an Argentinian businessman for weeks now. When she had finally accepted his offer of a date he could hardly believe his luck; and who cared if he had just had to sit through one of the most boring films ever (in black-and-white and with subtitles to boot)? Not even the events of the previous night could have put him off the opportunity of stealing one goodnight kiss from the seriously sexy Maria-Teresa!

"No, seriously," he smiled. "A beautiful girl like you shouldn't walk home on a night like this."

"You're forgetting a couple of things, Calvin," she said and snatched the umbrella off him. "This is *my* umbrella, and I'm a black-belt at judo!"

Calvin's face fell. "You are, huh?"

"That's right," Maria-Teresa said mock-threateningly, and then added good-naturedly, "So don't try anything on with me, OK? There's not a man alive who can get the better of me, *comprende*?"

"*Si*," said Calvin, sadly philosophical, "*comprendo* ..."

Maria-Teresa smiled. "Good! Well, if that's understood, then you can kiss me goodnight."

"*I can*?" Calvin could hardly believe his luck.

He reached down and pressed his lips against Maria-Teresa's, who responded with equal ardour. She tasted of mint, and vanilla, and she pressed her body close to his.

Finally she broke off the clinch. "Good night, Calvin," she breathed huskily.

"You've got to go, huh?"

"'Fraid so."

She turned around and then stopped, as if considering something. Eventually she said, "Calvin, I've really enjoyed this evening."

"So have I."

"*Really* enjoyed it," she said. "When I first met you I thought you were a bit of a fake. You were always following Jeff around, even hero-worshipping him—"

Dammit! thought Calvin angrily. *Why does he always have to find his way into every conversation I ever have with a girl! He's dead, for God's sake!*

"It seemed that all you wanted to be was another Jeff Rawlinson, to copy everything he did," Maria-Teresa continued. "That's why I've always stayed clear of you in the past."

"Hey, I'm a sweetie!" Calvin joked.

"Yes, you are," she said seriously and then smiled. "You're not like Jeff and you shouldn't try to be like him. I . . . knew Jeff . . . and once you scratched below the surface, once you saw beneath his good looks and his charm, he wasn't a nice person to know. He treated the girls he went out with just like trophies to wear on his arm. And once he got bored with one, he'd dump her straight away for another. He was a nasty piece of work, Calvin."

"We weren't exactly the best of friends, you know," Calvin said.

"I'm not surprised," she said. "Because when you scratch deep beneath *your* surface, there's a really nice and caring guy to be found there."

73

By now Calvin was feeling extremely embarrassed: the truth often did that to him.

Finally he said, "May I see you again, Maria-Teresa?"

"Just you try and stop me from seeing you again!" she grinned. "What are you doing tomorow night?"

"Monday?" Nothing," he said.

"Then it's a date—Tokyo Joe's tomorrow night at eight o'clock." She kissed him once more on the lips. "*Buenas noches*, Calvin."

"*Buenas noches*, Maria-Teresa."

She waved goodbye to him, and started walking down the rainy street which ran along the edge of the Heath. "I'll see you tomorrow, *si*?" she called back.

"*Si*," he said. "And take care, sweetheart."

"I will," she said and walked off down the road. Calvin watched her for a moment and then, whistling happily to himself, he went back to his car and drove away.

Maria-Teresa smiled: she liked Calvin a lot, and she hoped to see more of him. She looked up into the sky; the rain was coming down even more heavily now, and the raindrops were pounding noisily off the top of her umbrella. She quickened her pace, eager to be home in the warm and the dry.

"*Sweetheart . . . sweetheart . . .*"

Maria-Teresa stopped and looked at the buses on her right-hand side. In the shadows she couldn't see anything.

"Calvin, is that you?" she asked nervously.

"Sweetheart . . . sweetheart . . . "

"Calvin, if this is your idea of a joke then it's not funny."

There was no reply.

Maria-Teresa began to walk off again when an arm lunged out of the bushes and grabbed her. She tried to struggle but her feet slipped in the mud and she fell back into the bushes, their thorns slashing and ripping her face.

"Welcome back, sweetheart," oozed the voice, and Maria-Teresa looked up at the maniacally grinning face of her attacker.

"Santa Maria! she gasped in horror. "It cannot be you!"

"Oh yes it can! he laughed. *"Pleasant dreams . . . sweetheart . . . "*

Chapter 7

Calvin, Francesca, Murphy and Jean-Pierre all looked gloomily at each other as Mr Chippenham strode into the chemistry lab and slammed the door behind him. He was carrying a pile of schoolbooks in his arm and he threw them angrily down onto his teacher's desk before glaring at the assembled members of his class.

"Uh-oh," Calvin said to the others, "guess who's got that Monday morning feeling?"

"Either that," said Francesca, "or he's just finished marking last week's homework."

Chippenham regarded the class as though he was studying a particularly nasty growth in a test-tube. He had never made it a secret that he despised most of the students he taught; after all, as far as he was concerned, they were all a bunch of no-good rich kids who had everything handed to them on a silver platter. He had had to work damn hard to get where he was now, he thought resentfully, and even then his annual salary probably didn't come anywhere near the allowances his spoilt students got.

Finally he spoke.

"I have been the assistant chemistry master at

Castlemare High for eleven years," he began, and his voice was trembling with emotion. "And never in all my years here have I seen such sheer unadulterated claptrap as you have presented to me and dared to call homework!"

"You were right, Frannie," Calvin whispered philosophically. "He has marked the homework!"

"You are idiots, fools, every last one of you!" Chippenham thundered. "The material you have given in to me isn't even worthy of kindergarten children! Even you——" and here he turned to Francesca——"have let me down this time!"

Francesca moved uncomfortably in her seat; she knew that Chippenham regarded her as his prize student. Suddenly she regretted not asking for her mother's help on the weekend project Chippenham had set them.

Jean-Pierre stood up, a little nervously. "With respect, sir," he said, "it was a particularly difficult piece of homework——"

By his side, Calvin groaned. Jean-Pierre hadn't been at Castlemare long enough to have discovered that when Chippenham was throwing a tantrum it was best to let him ride it out.

"I beg your pardon?" the teacher growled at Jean-Pierre.

"I said it was a very difficult project, sir," Jean-Pierre said, now wishing that he hadn't started the conversation at all. "I'm sure that we all did the best we could—but we only had two days to write an essay that, by rights, needed at least five days' research."

Chippenham stared at Jean-Pierre as if he couldn't believe what he had just heard.

"By rights? And what do you know about rights?" demanded Chippenham.

"Sorry, sir? I don't understand."

"You come from nothing less than a tin-pot little country, ruled by superstition and fear," said Chippenham, who had always been proud of his true-blue British ancestry. "What do you know about rights, or modern-day science for that matter? Why, only a matter of decades ago your ancestors were living in what could be regarded as little more than barbarism."

A deathly hush descended on the laboratory and even Chippenham realised that, not for the first time, he might have let his temper get the better of him.

Jean-Pierre stared hatefully at his teacher, but, unlike Chippenham, he kept his cool.

"Sir, my people are the descendents of a great and noble race," he said flatly. "And I ask you to retract that last statement."

Now he's really asking for it! thought Francesca, but still felt pride for her classmate.

"You insolent young—"

Chippenham brought his fist crashing down to the desk in an effort to control himself. Everyone in the class looked at each other knowingly: Chippenham had just stopped himself from saying one of the few words that would have meant his instant dismissal from Castlemare High.

If there was anything Miss Greystone, the Principal, hated most in the world it was racism. For a start, in a multi-racial school such as Castlemare, any hint of racism would mean at least a hundred parents taking their children away—and, along with them, their sizeable tuition fees.

"Your work was particularly bad, Denfer, as it has been for most of the term," Chippenham said, then finally regained his composure. "Now—would you please all open your textbooks . . ."

"Well done, Jean-Pierre," said Calvin.

"Yes, it took some guts to stand up to Chippenham like that," agreed Murphy.

"He should not have said such untruths about my people," said Jean-Pierre, and they were both surprised at the unconcealed venom in the voice of the normally placid and easy-going Haitian.

"He will pay for having said such things . . ."

"Penny for them?"

Calvin looked up from his bowl of steaming Japanese green tea to see Murphy's grinning face.

"You've been staring into your tea for the past hour or so," she said. "This is Tokyo Joe's, not a funeral parlour!" She nodded over to a group of their friends at a table in the corner. "Why don't you come over and join us?"

"That's kind of you, Murphy, but I'm waiting for someone, you see . . ."

"Aha!" said Murphy, delighted at having stumbled upon a piece of gossip. "A hot date! And what time was she supposed to meet you?"

Calvin looked at his Swatch. "Eight o'clock," he said. It was now nine-thirty.

"Face it, Calvin, she's stood you up—it can

happen even to sure-fire studs like you, you know!" she said flippantly, and dragged him over to the others. "Who was the miserable no-show anyway?"

"Maria-Teresa . . ."

"There you go!" said Murphy, as if that suddenly explained everything. "She's a Latin! They're notoriously unreliable!"

"Thank you very much," Calvin said wryly, and accepted a proffered china mug of hot sake from Kim.

"What's the crisis?" the Japanese girl asked.

"Lover-boy's just been stood up," Murphy said bluntly, but not maliciously.

"Well, maybe she's been delayed?" Kim suggested.

Calvin shook his head. "I phoned her but there was no reply."

"Not even from her parents?" Murphy asked, a sudden edge in her voice.

"She has her own flat in Highgate," Calvin said. "They bought it for her last year."

"Well, I'm sure there's a simple explanation," said Murphy, and picked up a piece of sushi with her chopsticks and popped it into Calvin's mouth. "In the meantime eat on this—and I promise you that it won't give you food poisoning!"

Murphy's flipness was for Calvin's benefit, for a dull doubt was nagging away at the back of her mind. She and Maria-Teresa were in the same language class, and the young Argentinian girl hadn't turned up for the lesson this afternoon either. She thoughtfully stroked the Damballah pendant that Jean-Pierre had given her the previous day.

Then Murphy chuckled, and stared accusingly at the bottle of sake which Tokyo Joe himself had bought for their group. She had obviously drunk too much, and it had all gone to her head. She was imagining things, of course. Like she said, there had to be a simple explanation, hadn't there?

Suddenly the door to the bar was thrown open and Francesca rushed in. Her normally carefully styled red hair was wet and bedraggled from the rain outside, and the raw rings around her eyes showed that she had been crying.

Calvin instantly stood up and offered her his seat. "What is it, Frannie?" he asked. "What's wrong, sweetheart?"

Francesca struggled to get her breath back: she had run all the way to the bar where she knew her friends would be.

"This," she said, and threw an object onto the table. "I found it on the doorstep when I returned home this evening."

It was a rag doll, very crudely made, but, with its distinctive shock of red hair, it was plain that it was meant to be a representation of Francesca.

There was a long, rusty needle stuck through its stomach.

Mr Chippenham stumbled to the top of the stairs and tried to locate the lock of the door to his flat. It had been a long and tiring day, and he had drunk several double whiskies too many at The

Cricketers, the pub many of the staff at Castlemare frequented after school.

After several abortive attempts he managed to insert his key into the lock and entered his poky little flat at the top of a terraced house in Tufnell Park, a slightly down-at-heel area just south of Hampstead Heath. Not for the first time he forgot to shut the door in his drunkenness.

His three tiny rooms were a stark contrast to the wealth and luxury in which many of the students he taught lived. The little blighters didn't know they were born, he grumbled to himself; and him having served his country in the Second World War! There was no justice or decency left in the world, that was for sure!

He threw his briefcase down on the threadbare sofa and thought about doing some marking. No, he decided, that could wait till tomorrow morning when he'd do it on the bus into school; after all, that was when he'd marked his A-level class's weekend homework.

Thinking of that weekend homework reminded him of Jean-Pierre. The Haitian had particularly annoyed him, and had ruined his entire day. It was a disgrace, thought Chippenham, that someone like that should stand up to him. The chemistry teacher was a racist, pure and simple. When the first Pakistani had opened the first corner shop in his road over twenty-five years ago, it was then that Mr Chippenham had decided that the country he had fought for so hard was finally going well and truly to the dogs.

The chemistry teacher flopped back into his

favourite armchair, the one he had bought in a furniture sale in the mid-1970s, and decided on a twenty-minute nap.

Three hours later he woke up with a splitting headache. He glanced over at the clock on the mantelpiece: one o'clock in the morning. Once again he cursed himself for drinking too much and vowed that tomorrow would be different. What was particularly galling was that there were a couple of experiments he had wanted to conduct at home tonight. Mr Chippenham had very little social life (apart from The Cricketers, of course) so he had brought many bottles of chemicals home from Castlemare, and he often conducted experiments here at home late into the night. It was strictly against the rules of course, but that had never bothered him.

Well, not tonight, old chap! he told himself. What he needed, he decided, was a nice stiff nightcap, and then off to bed.

He started to get up and discovered that he couldn't. His arms were bound fast to his side, and his legs were tied to his favourite armchair with a length of kitchen cord.

"Naughty Mr Chippenham," came a crusty voice from behind him. "Don't you know that all that drinking's bad for you?"

Chippenham tried to turn round but found that that a cord around his forehead was holding his head firm as well. There was a terrible smell in the room, like putrefying flesh.

"Who is it? Who's there?" he asked, and streams of sweat began to pour down his brow.

"Don't you know?" came the voice again. "Maybe you should just call me Baron Samedi . . ."

"Baron who? I don't understand what you're saying!"

Baron Samedi, teacher. The angel of death . . ."

"Look, take what you want," Chippenham said. "Only leave me alone!"

"Oh there's nothing that *you* have that I could possibly want," the voice sneered.

"Then what do you want?" Even beneath his bonds Chippenham was quaking with fear.

"You're a sad little man, Chippenham, did you know that? You're not even a very good chemistry teacher either. You're also a very nasty little racist."

"I assure you that I have no idea what you mean . . ."

"Don't give me that!" said the voice, and Chippenham could feel its hot and fetid breath on the back of his neck. He felt it's hands touch his shoulders, and then he felt something *wriggling* on the bare flesh of his neck.

"Your racism's an illness, Chippenham," the voice continued. "And, just like any other illness, it's got to be cured."

The voice moved away from him, and Chippenham could hear someone moving about in the kitchen. Then he heard the soft padding sound of feet as the voice returned to the living-room.

"You're ill, Mr Chippenham," the voice said. "And now it's time to take your medicine."

A dirty and bloody hand reached out from behind him. The hand was carrying a metal dessert spoon into which had been poured a colourless but pungent liquid.

"Come on, Mr Chippenham, take your medicine like a good little racist should . . ."

The chemistry teacher clamped his mouth shut. Chippenham had recognised the liquid's distinctive aroma: it was the stink of rotten eggs.

"Tut-tut-tut," chuckled the voice. "We are being uncooperative, tonight, aren't we?"

Another hand came out from behind Chippenham and squeezed hard on his nose, making it impossible for him to breathe without opening his mouth.

He was forced to open his mouth and, the instant that he did, the spoon and its vicious contents were rammed into his mouth.

Chippenham choked and spluttered as another, and another, and yet another spoonful were poured down his throat.

The liquid seared and scorched his mouth, his throat, his windpipe, his stomach, and it seeped into his liver, his pancreas, his kidneys, into every crevice and corner of his body.

But by this time Mr Chippenham had been long dead, which was hardly surprising.

The human body, after all, is not designed to consume over a litre and a half of undiluted sulphuric acid.

Chapter 8

Calvin tossed and turned in his bed, unable to get to sleep. In his dreams he could hear familiar voices calling out his name, crying out for his help. But when he tried to reach out for the people behind the voices they vanished like mist.

Blearily he opened his eyes and looked at his bedside clock: 0346 on a Thursday morning.

Realising that he'd never get back to sleep now, he got out of bed and threw his dressing-gown over his shoulder. He switched on the bedroom light and looked at himself in the mirror. He looked like death—hardly the handsome hunk who was fancied, so he liked to believe, by at least half the female population of Castlemare.

He sat back down on the bed and sank his face in his hands. Yesterday, Wednesday, had been the latest in a series of days which had been getting worse and worse.

He had phoned Maria-Teresa on Tuesday, to see why the hell she had stood him up, and there had been no reply. After trying unsuccessfully again on Wednesday, he had thought of ringing her parents. He had worked his considerable charms on the school secretary and had just managed to get the Argentinian girl's parents' number when they had actually rung *him*, demanding to speak to her.

It seemed that they had heard that their daughter liked him a lot—even in the circumstances this boosted his macho ego!—and thought that she might be staying at his place, as they couldn't contact her at her own flat.

And then Police Sergeant Evans had come around—in the middle of the chemistry class for God's sake!

Calvin had had to ask to be excused the class, much to the annoyance of Mrs Jenner, who was standing in for Chippenham in his absence. When she had demanded a reason, he had reluctantly said that he had been requested to "help the police with their enquiries".

And everyone knew what that really meant . . .

Calvin had been the last person to see Maria-Teresa, Evans had explained to him, and he needed to know where Calvin thought she might have been heading for when she had left him on Monday night outside the cinema.

After Calvin had told Evans and the girl's worried parents that he thought she had gone straight home, and that she had apparently stood him up at Tokyo Joe's the following night, Maria-Teresa had been officially declared a Missing Person.

So was it any wonder that he couldn't get to sleep tonight!

Tap-tap-tap.

Calvin looked around, trying to identify the source of the noise. Then he heard a voice.

"Calvin . . . Calvin . . ."

It was a woman's voice. And it spoke with the faintest trace of a Latin American accent.

He raced over to his bedroom window and ripped open the curtains. His bedroom was on the ground floor, but there was no one outside, nothing except the endlessly pouring rain, its pounding on the driveway seeming to mock him.

Calvin snarled angrily and, without bothering to draw the curtains, flung himself back onto the bed where he fell into a fitful sleep. But for the rest of the night he was plagued by one recurring image: Maria-Teresa's face, as white as bone, and her fingers tapping against his window-pane, begging, pleading to be let in.

In spite of her unnatural paleness, she was still as beautiful as she was when Calvin had said good-bye to her last Monday. Her lips were still as full and sexy as they had been when he had kissed her goodnight, her teeth were still as white as pearls, and her eyes, although their sparkle was somewhat dulled, still shone with a ready intelligence and wit.

But there were maggots in her hair.

Mrs Jenner beamed as she handed back the homework she had set her class the previous day. She was especially pleased with the work her class had done; after all, Mr Chippenham's class did have a reputation for not being a group of high achievers.

But Chippenham had set this test himself and most of these marks were first-class; for a moment she wondered whether the fault lay not in his students but in Chippenham's own teaching and marking methods.

After all, it was an open secret in the classroom that Chippenham did like the odd drink now and then. Maybe it was a lucky accident for the whole class that the old codger had fallen mysteriously ill, and that she had been assigned as a supply teacher until his return.

"Well done—" she read the unfamiliar name on the top of the paper as she handed it out—"Calvin. And well done you too, Bernadette."

"Murphy," Murphy corrected her automatically, and then turned to Calvin.

"You look like death!"

"So would you if you'd been up half the night."

"Lucky you."

"Not funny, sweetheart."

Mrs Jenner looked askance at the class and waved an answer sheet in the air. "Francesca Barton?" she asked.

Murphy raised her hand. "I'll take that, Mrs Jenner" she said. "Francesca's ill today."

"I am sorry!" Mrs Jenner sympathised and handed the paper over to Murphy. Nothing serious, I hope?"

Murphy shrugged. "Just some stomach pains," she said.

Mrs Jenner turned away, and looked at the name of the top of the next answer sheet.

"Jean-Pierre Denfer?" she asked and handed the paper to Jean-Pierre when he put his hand up.

"An excellent piece of work, *Monsieur Denfer*,"

she said, and Jean-Pierre beamed. "Your A-minus is well-deserved."

"Thank you, Mrs Jenner," Jean-Pierre beamed. "I've been working especially hard lately."

Calvin and Murphy exchanged astonished looks.

"Jean-Pierre?" asked Murphy in amazement. "Only a few days ago he was getting D-pluses if he was lucky! And now A-minuses?"

Calvin shrugged. "Maybe he's been working as hard as he's said he has been—"

The door to the classroom opened, and Miss Greystone, the Principal, walked in. She was dressed all in black and there was a sombre and mournful look about her.

"Mrs Jenner, if I may address the class for a moment?" she asked.

The supply teacher was just as surprised at the unexpected intrusion as everyone else, and willingly let the Principal talk to the class.

Miss Greystone took a deep breath and began. "I'm sure you've all been wondering what has been wrong with Mr Chippenham . . ."

Calvin, Murphy and Jean-Pierre looked at each other; to be perfectly honest, the thought had never crossed their minds. They had just been relieved that Mrs Jenner, a notoriously soft touch on the teaching staff, had been chosen to take over from him.

Miss Greystone lowered her eyes so that she did not to have to look at the students. "It is my sad duty to have to inform you that Mr Chippenham was found dead in his flat this morning." She shuddered as she remembered the police bringing her to the squalid little flat to identify his body. "He had been murdered."

A murmur of excitement arose from the class, as a barrage of questions was fired at the Principal.

"How? Why? When? Who?"

"It seems that he disturbed a burglar," Miss Greystone continued. "Or at least that is what the police are saying . . ."

"A burglar?" Murphy was confused. "But I wouldn't have thought that Chips—I mean, Mr Chippenham—had anything worth stealing . . ."

"Unless you count this term's exam papers," Calvin said flippantly and then instantly regretted it as Miss Greystone glared at him. "Sorry, Miss Greystone, my big mouth again . . ."

"How did you know about that?"

"Know about what?"

"The only thing missing from Mr Chippenham's flat were the answers to this week's chemistry exam," she said slowly.

Calvin suddenly felt the eyes of the entire class turn on him. He looked around nervously. "Hey, what are you suggesting?" he asked. "You all don't think that I had anything to do with Chips's murder . . . do you . . .?"

Miss Greystone didn't reply. Calvin lifted up his marked test paper. "Look! A B! If I'd lifted the answers surely I'd have made sure I got a better grade than that!"

"It's perfectly all right, Calvin," Miss Greystone finally replied. "I am not accusing you of anything at all."

Calvin felt the tension ease a little. Maye he was

just being paranoid; no one would really consider him capable of murder, would they?

"Hell, if I was really doing the job right I'd've made sure that I scored a B-plus at the very least—or maybe even an A-minus . . ."

His voice tailed away as both he and Murphy looked at Jean-Pierre, the student who, no matter how hard he had worked before, had always only ever scored Ds.

And what mark had Jean-Pierre just received for his chemistry test?

An A-minus . . .

This time the dream was stronger, more real than ever before. Maria-Teresa was bashing her tiny little fists at Calvin's bedroom window, begging to be let in. She was crying, but the tears that poured from her eyes were not tears of salt-water but tears of blood.

There was a name that she was calling out. Not Calvin's name, but a name which obviously invoked terror in her heart. Calvin struggled to hear her through the glass.

"The Baron, Calvin, save me from the Baron!"

"The Baron?" said Calvin. "I don't understand. Tell me what's wrong, Maria-Teresa! Who is the Baron?"

"The Dark Lord," said a voice in Calvin's dream, a low guttural voice that seemed strangely familiar. "The Obi-man, Calvin . . ."

"Obi-man?"

"You know what 'obeah' is, don't you, Calvin?"

In his bed Calvin shook his head wildly. And

yet . . . and yet he recalled hearing the word spoken before . . . by Kim, wasn't it?

"He's got me, Calvin!" screamed Maria-Teresa. "The Obi-man's got me!"

"The Obi-man? Who is he?" Calvin yelled out. "Who is the Baron?"

"Why, that's me," said the voice. "Baron Samedi, of course, the God of the Dead . . ."

Samedi? The word was familiar and then Calvin remembered that it was the French word for "Saturday". And who amongst all his friends had a mother tongue that was French?

Jean-Pierre, of course.

Chapter 9

There was no doubt about it, thought Kim, this was definitely her favourite day in the year: 31 October, Hallowe'en. The fact that this year it also fell on a Friday was even better—that would mean that she could stay out all night at one of the many Hallowe'en parties her friends were having, and not have to worry about getting up early the next morning for school. Even this early in the morning she was excited about the events of the coming night.

Kim loved all the spookiness associated with Hallowe'en: the lighted pumpkins, the dressing up, the darkened corners at the Hallowe'en parties where she could kiss and cuddle with the latest hunk from the sixth form. She didn't really believe all that stuff about witches and hobgoblins roaming abroad that night, but if it served as a good excuse for a party then who was she to complain?

She glanced at her bedside clock: it had just turned seven-thirty in the morning and she would soon have to be making her way to school. Looking at herself in the mirror she decided that she looked pretty neat: a baggy white Comme des Garçons T-shirt, black Lycra leggings and a wonderful black frockcoat that she had picked up in an Oxfam shop in South Kensington a few months ago. To finish it all off she perched on the top of her head a battered old opera hat of her father's.

She looked at herself admiringly. There was no doubt about it, she decided, she had style. Dressed in her black and second-hand clothes she looked like a grunge princess, a female Charlie Chaplin with miles more style and sophistication. If this didn't get the boys noticing her today then nothing would.

"You look very pretty today."

Kim smiled. "Thanks, dad," she said, without turning around.

"And how fitting for Hallowe'en—dressed all in black," he continued. "You've really dressed for the occasion, *sweetheart*."

Kim started, then slowly turned around. The person standing in the door admiring her was not her father. She felt her breath catch in her throat.

"My God, we were right," she said. "You *are* alive . . ."

The foul-smelling creature advanced on her; to her horror Kim found that she was unable to move.

"Oh no," it said. "You were very, very wrong . . ." It lifted up its arm, pulling back the sleeve of its baseball jacket to reveal a bone-white and emaciated arm. It was encrusted with sores out of which seemed to ooze hundreds and hundreds of maggots.

"As you see," the voice continued to rasp, "I am very, very dead . . ."

"But that's impossible," Kim breathed. "The dead can't walk . . ."

For a scarcely perceptible second the creature paused, and from its cracked and peeling lips there came what to Kim sounded almost like a sob of regret.

"And that's where you're wrong again, sweetheart," it continued. "It's not impossible at all. It's obeah . . ."

"Obeah . . ." Kim finally remembered where she had seen the word before. It had been in one of her dictionaries of mythology and superstitions. "Witchcraft," she said. "Magic . . ."

The creature shook its head,. "Not any kind of witchcraft, sweetheart," it laughed. "Not just any kind of magic. A special kind of witchcraft, a special kind of magic. A magic that is practised on one island in particular . . ."

Kim nodded, as suddenly several things became clear to her. "I know . . . Haiti . . ."

"That's right, Kim, voodoo," the creature congratulated her. "And now it's your turn, sweetheart, now it's your turn to become one of us . . ."

"Voodoo," said Calvin, his voice full of hate. "We should have known all along."

"You should not talk about the religion of my ancestors like that . . ."

"I don't give a toss about your religion anymore!" Calvin cried, and was about to hit Jean-Pierre when Murphy pulled him back.

"I don't understand what you are trying to say, Calvin," Jean-Pierre said.

"Then why have you been avoiding us all day?" he demanded. "Why did we have to wait until—" he looked at his Swatch—"until six o'clock in the evening before we could track you down in the senior common room?"

"I told you," said Jean-Pierre, "I have been studying all day . . . I must improve my grades . . ."

"Like you improved your chemistry grades," the young American continued. "Admit it, Jean-Pierre, you'd never get an A-minus through your own work. Not unless you stole the exam papers!"

Jean-Pierre was silent for a moment as the full implication of what Calvin had just said was brought home to him.

"You think I killed Chippenham?"

"Why not?" asked Calvin. "You had the motive. He was a pathetic little racist who tried to make a fool of you. You had everything to gain by killing him!"

Murphy urged Calvin to be quiet but the American would no longer listen to reason. "In fact, I wouldn't be surprised if you had something to do with Maria-Teresa's disappearance."

"Calvin, you are upset," Jean-Pierre said. "I know what Maria-Teresa meant to you."

"I've been doing some research in the library since yesterday's chemistry class, Jean-Pierre," Calvin said. "And I've learnt all about dolls with pins stuck in them. About chicken carcasses left on doorsteps . . ."

Jean-Pierre eyed Calvin warily. "And?"

"And I've learnt that they're all tricks used by voodoo priests to scare people, to bring them into line," he said. "To make them think that the gods of voodoo will destroy them . . ."

Jean-Pierre looked pleadingly at Murphy. "You can't believe him, Murphy," he appealed. "That cockerel at your doorstep wasn't put there by me!"

Murphy looked at him strangely.

"What cockerel, Jean-Pierre?" she asked, and Jean-Pierre mentally kicked himself as he remembered that he had kept the discovery of the dead bird away from the Irish girl.

"You're different from us, Jean-Pierre," Calvin said slowly.

"That's what Chippenham thought too," Jean-Pierre reminded him, giving Calvin a second's pause for thought.

"We don't really know you at all," he continued nonetheless. "You've kept yourself to yourself ever since you came to Castlemare . . ."

"I told you—I've been studying all that time—"

"And you know what? It's very funny, but all the trouble at Castlemare only started when you arrived here—"

Murphy grabbed Calvin's arm. "What are you saying, Calvin?" she asked, although she feared she already knew the answer.

"Sophie Ashford's death . . . Claire's murder . . . the voodoo warnings . . . Maria-Teresa's disappearance . . . even your food-poisoning, Murphy, and Frannie's illness—they've only happened since this—he looked despisingly at Jean-Pierre—"since *this* came to Castlemare—"

He lunged at the Haitian, who backed away

from him. Murphy grabbed Calvin and tried to hold him back.

"Calvin! Stop it!"

"He's a killer, Murphy!" Calvin yelled.

"I do not kill!" Jean-Pierre shouted, and his voice was suddenly powerful and commanding. "There is a greater evil at work here!"

Calvin and Murphy looked curiously at the young Haitian. In a reflex action Murphy nervously touched her pendant of the Snake God.

"Why would I wish to harm Sophie, or Maria-Teresa?" he asked. "I hardly knew them!"

Even Calvin didn't have an answer to that one.

"If all these 'incidents' are the work of one person then there must be a connection between them all," Jean-Pierre continued. "Something which they all have in common . . ."

"But what?" asked Calvin, who was struggling to remain calm. "Sophie and Claire couldn't stand each other. They had absolutely nothing in common at all."

"Except their taste in boys," said Murphy.

"*What*?"

"They both went out with Jeff Rawlinson," said Murphy. "And he dumped both of them, just like he dumped Frannie . . ."

Damm Jeff Rawlinson! thought Calvin angrily. *When am I ever going to escape from his shadow?*

"Maria-Teresa said she knew Jeff . . ." Calvin said unwillingly and then sneered. "That's rubbish, Murphy, and you know it. If it was true then why were you attacked?"

Murphy lowered her eyes. "Ah, well . . ."

"Murphy, not you as well?"

"It was just one night, Calvin," she said, "and I can't say I'm proud of it . . ."

"But when?"

"The Christmas party. You'd drunk too much wine and eaten too much Christmas cake, so you wouldn't remember . . ."

To hell with Jeff! thought Calvin. *Wasn't there a single girl at Castlemare who his pretty-boy rival hadn't gone out with?*

"That doesn't explain Chippenham's murder though," he pointed out.

"Unless it was a red herring," said Murphy.

"A what?" asked Jean-Pierre urgently.

"A red herring," repeated Murphy. "It's an English expression. It means something which is designed to lead you away from the truth. Maybe Chippenham was killed to divert attention away from the real murderer, and to put the blame for his murder on someone else—on you, for instance."

Strangely Jean-Pierre was suddenly not interested in Murphy's suggestion that he might be innocent.

"A red herring . . ." he repeated.

"That's right," said Calvin, intrigued. He searched around for a French approximation. "*Un hareng rouge?*"

"*Oui, oui, oui,*" said Jean-Pierre, "*je sais . . . un poisson . . .* A fish . . ."

Suddenly he looked very worried indeed, as if the pieces of a jigsaw were finally fitting together into a picture he had dreaded ever seeing again.

"Let us say that Chippenham is a 'red herring'," he suggested finally. "If that is so then the only thing which links Murphy and all the other girls together is—"

"I know," Calvin said resentfully. "Jeff Rawlinson!" He turned to Murphy. "I told Frannie that I'd seen him, that he was still alive!"

Jean-Pierre looked at Murphy, and there was a worried look in his eyes. "Well, Murphy, is that possible?" he asked, in a tone which suggested that he already knew what her answer would be.

Murphy shook her head. "I'm sorry, boys," she said. "It's a nice theory but it doesn't work. You might have seen someone, Calvin, but it certainly wasn't Jeff Rawlinson. Jeff is dead."

Jean-Pierre looked searchingly at Murphy. "How can you be so sure?" he demanded.

"Easy," she said. "I went to his funeral, Jean-Pierre. I saw his coffin being put into the family crypt. There is no way that Jeff Rawlinson is still alive!"

Jean-Pierre froze, and his eyes stared wildly ahead. He was shivering and a cold sheen of sweat had appeared on his brow. Even Calvin was concerned for him.

"Hey, man, what's up?" he asked. "What's the problem?"

"It is as I had feared," Jean-Pierre said. "I had hoped that I was wrong and that is why I have kept silent for so long." He turned to Murphy and Calvin. "A terrible evil has followed me from Haiti, my friends. An unspeakable curse has descended upon Castlemare High."

"What is it, Jean-Pierre?" asked Murphy. "What are you talking about?"

There was a great sadness in Jean-Pierre's voice as he pronounced the word, the word that both Murphy and Calvin were by now almost half-expecting.

"Zombies."

Chapter 10

"*Zombies*? You are out of your freaking tree, Jean-Pierre!" protested Calvin. "This is real life—not some Hammer Horror movie."

"But zombies are real life, Calvin," Jean-Pierre insisted.

"Oh yeah, sure!" he scoffed. "Like leprechauns, and vampires, and not walking under ladders, and fairies at the bottom of my garden!"

"Do not speak lightly of the religion of my ancestors, Calvin," Jean-Pierre warned.

"OK, man, I'm sorry," said Calvin. "But zombies? They belong in some late-night horror movie on TV!"

Jean-Pierre shook his head and repeated: "Zombies exist."

Calvin continued to scoff, but Murphy looked challengingly at Jean-Pierre.

"How?" she asked.

"Fish," came back the enigmatic answer.

Murphy and Calvin stared at each other. What was Jean-Pierre talking about?

"Fish," he said again, then allowed himself the small luxury of a chuckle. "Not your red herring,

Murphy, not even your trendy sushi; but the puffer fish."

Murphy remembered being in Tokyo Joe's a couple of weeks ago and remembered Kim talking about the puffer fish. She'd called it one of the most poisonous creatures in the whole world.

"The puffer fish is a source of tetrodotoxin," Jean-Pierre said, as if that explained everything.

"So?" asked Calvin.

"So tetrodotoxin is one of the strongest poisons known to mankind," Jean-Pierre continued. "It can kill a man as easily as this—" He clicked his fingers.

"You're saying that Sophie and Claire were poisoned?" asked Calvin.

"No, quite the reverse," he said. "Tetrodotoxin has other uses too. When applied in the correct quantities, by a skilled chemist for example, it can produce the appearance of death. The bodily functions of the victim will cease but he—or she—will not die. They will become a zombie, a senseless, unthinking, unfeeling creature, a mere mockery of their former selves. When he—or she—'awakens' from their death-like sleep they will obey whatever commands are given to them . . ."

"But Claire's throat was cut," said Calvin. "She's dead and buried. And Sophie died of a heart attack . . ."

"I did not say that *they* were zombies, Calvin," Jean-Pierre said meaningfully.

"Wait a minute," said Murphy as she tried to take it all in. "You're saying that Calvin actually did see Jeff . . . and that Jeff was a zombie . . ."

"Someone affected by a carefully controlled

amount of tetrodotoxin, yes," said Jean-Pierre, and then smiled: "Or, if you like, in the parlance of my own people, a zombie."

"And Jeff decided to kill off his former girl-friends one by one" Calvin finished.

"No!" said Jean-Pierre, with feeling. "The zom-bie-creature is innocent! It cannot think for itself. It must be controlled by another—by a *hungan* or a *mambo*."

"By a what?" asked Murphy.

"The *hungan* and the *mambo* are the witch-king and the witch-queen of the voodoo religion," explained Jean-Pierre. "Only they can control the zombie. Only they can make the dead rise from their graves!"

A ghastly chill settled over the room. "Only the *hungan* and the *mambo*, the servants of Baron Samedi, can control the zombie-creature," Jean-Pierre said.

"Who?" demanded Calvin.

"Baron Samedi," repeated Jean-Pierre. "The voodoo god of death."

It was the name Maria-Teresa had used in Cal-vin's dream.

"It can't be," he whispered, but Jean-Pierre mis-understood his meaning.

"I assure you he is the death-god," he main-tained. "If you do not believe me, then ask Kim."

"Kim?" said Murphy. "What do you know about her?"

"Murphy, I don't understand" said Jean-Pierre and even Calvin loked curiously at the Irish girl.

"She didn't turn up for class this morning, Jean-

Pierre," Murphy said. "I tried ringing her at home but there was no reply. Even the answermachine was switched off."

"I'm sure she's all right," said Jean-Pierre with a conviction he didn't feel.

"Yeah," said Calvin uneasily. "You know what Kim's like. It's Hallowe'en! She's probably been spending most of today getting ready for one of tonight's parties."

Murphy took a deep breath. Kim had made her promise never to tell anyone else, but . . .

"You don't understand, guys," she began. "Kim . . . she . . . well, after Frannie . . ."

"What is it, sweetheart?" demanded Calvin.

"Well, after Frannie and Jeff split up, she was Jeff's girlfriend . . ."

"Then may the great Lord Damballah preserve her soul," said Jean-Pierre.

Chapter 11

The rain poured down onto the gravestones and mausoleums of Highgate Cemetery, turning the already treacherous ground into a moving morass of mud and mire. Thunder crashed ominously, and in the sky overhead ink-black storm clouds covered the face of the moon. There were no stars. The only illumination was the ice-brilliant lightning as it forked and streaked evilly through the sky, bathing the graveyard in its own eerie blue light.

The wind seemed to have been roused and excited by the unholy chaos all around it and it was howling through the trees, breaking off smaller branches, and swaying the larger ones to and fro. Dry autumnal leaves were swept all about the place, caught up in the gale, and little animals skittered and fell about in the mud, desperately searching out a place in which to shelter from the storm. It was as if all Hell had broken loose in the cemetery: it was truly the Hallowe'en to end all Hallowe'ens.

The centre of the chaos, if the omnipresent mayhem could be said to have a centre, seemed to focus itself on one tomb. By the Rawlinson family mausoleum stood a solitary figure. Silhouetted by the lightning flare it could be seen to be wearing a long dark coat and a top hat, bizarrely looking like someone ready to go off and visit the opera, if it had not been for the large grave-digger's shovel on which it was leaning. It seemed oblivious to the wind and the rain, as if it was waiting for something.

Or someone . . .

Calvin, Murphy and Jean-Pierre waded through the mud as they climbed the small hillock leading up to the Rawlinson tomb. Calvin looked accusingly at Jean-Pierre.

"We're crazy to be doing this!" he cried above the deafening sound of the thunder and the wind and the rain.

"No!" shouted Jean-Pierre. "The zombie is not our enemy! He must be saved!"

"*Saved*!" Calvin couldn't believe what he was hearing. "The guy's a killer, Jean-Pierre!"

"No!" Jean-Pierre said again. "The zombie is merely an instrument, a mindless creature that will obey the commands of its master. It is no more guilty of murder than a gun fired by a criminal. The real killer is the *hungan* or *mambo* who sends it out on its mission of evil!"

"Oh yeah?" said Calvin doubtfully. "Well, I've heard that you can't hypnotise people to do things they wouldn't normally do in real life"—

"The zombie is not 'hypnotised', Calvin."

Murphy could stand it no more.

"Will you two shut it!" she yelled. "If you don't

108

want to save Jeff, Calvin, then at least think of Maria-Teresa!"

"Hey, I didn't say that," Calvin said defensively.

"You've always hated Jeff!" she said. "He got all the girls you wanted, all the best modelling contracts, all the top grades. Admit it, Calvin, you were jealous of him. And all you really wanted was to be like him!"

"You're wrong . . ."

"Am I? Then why were you so glad when we all thought he'd died? Why were you so obsessed to prove that he really was dead? Heck, you even call everyone 'sweetheart' all the time, just because that's what Jeff always used to do!"

Calvin tried to answer back, and found that he couldn't: he knew that Murphy was right. And even though he hated Jeff, he knew that he couldn't let him remain dead if there was any chance of saving him or Maria-Teresa.

"My friends! Let us stop arguing amongst ourselves," said Jean-Pierre. "The real enemy is there!"

They all looked in the direction his finger was pointing. By the tomb they saw the strange top-hatted figure.

"Who is that?" asked Murphy, although she thought she already knew.

"The morning coat and the top hat means it can only be one person," said Jean-Pierre sombrely, a distinct tremble in his voice. "They are the raiments of Baron Samedi, the god of the dead."

"Don't be stupid!" said Murphy. "There's no such person."

She stepped forward to take a closer look. As she did so the lightning flashed, illuminating the face of the top-hatted figure.

"Kim!" Murphy screamed.

Kim turned towards Murphy and looked at her strangely, as if she didn't quite recognise her old schoolfriend.

"She is the *mambo*!" gasped Jean-Pierre. "The mistress of the zombies!"

"No!" cried Calvin. "Look at her eyes!"

Kim's eyes were just two large and empty whites; her pupils were nowhere to be seen. Her oriental complexion was pale, as pale as ash, and two large dark circles hung beneath her eyes.

"She's been turned into a zombie too," Jean-Pierre realised. "When will it all end?"

"Calvin? Calvin? Is that you?"

Calvin spun around on his heels, away from the tomb, and towards a large yew tree which was creaking and swaying in the wind. There, still in the dress she had worn on Sunday night, although it was now muddied and torn, was Maria-Teresa. He made to rush towards her, but Jean-Pierre held him back.

"Look at her, Calvin!" he said. "Look at her eyes! She has joined the league of the undead as well! She has become one of the walkers! She is a zombie!"

"Help me, Calvin," Maria-Teresa begged and reached out to the American with bleeding and grasping fingers. "Help me . . . I don't want to be dead . . ."

Calvin looked wildly, imploringly, at Jean-Pierre. "There must be something we can do!" he cried.

Jean-Pierre shook his head. "Their will has been taken from them. We can do nothing until their master appears."

Shocked by the appearance of two of her friends, literally more dead than alive, Murphy backed away from the tomb. She felt a hand touch her shoulder in a gesture which could have been described as tender were it not for the fact that the hand that touched her was crawling with maggots and worms.

"Hello again, sweetheart . . ."

Murphy tried to run, but Jeff was too strong for her.

He pulled her back, and she felt a long rusty knife being held to her throat. By the tomb Kim and Maria-Teresa hissed with delight: here was fine sport indeed!

"You scum!" cried Calvin, and made a movement towards him.

"One more move and she gets it!"

Jeff spat out the words, and Murphy nearly fainted as she smelt his fetid breath, that rank stink of corruption and putrefying flesh.

"What do you want, you filthy zombie!" barked Calvin. Jeff didn't reply, just laughed.

Jean-Pierre put a hand on Calvin's shoulder. In the midst of the storm it felt strangely calm and reassuring.

"Not a 'filthy zombie' Calvin," he said, more than loud enough for Jeff to hear him above the wail of the wind. "His name is Jeff. Jeff Rawlinson . . ."

And then to Calvin and Murphy's utter disbelief, Jean-Pierre walked calmly up to the zombie, his hand outstretched in a gesture of welcome.

"Hello, Jeff Rawlinson," he said pleasantly. "We don't know each other, but I'm sure we can be great friends, *Jeff*. My name is Jean-Pierre Denfer. And you, of course, are *Jeff Rawlinson*. That is right, isn't it, Jeff? *Jeff Rawlinson*."

Jean-Pierre stared at Jeff with an intensity that frightened even Murphy. The young Haitian had always come across to her before as being so innocuous; and yet here, in Highgate Cemetery, in the middle of this terrible storm, even with a knife at her neck, she was suddenly scared of Jean-Pierre. He seemed someone who could be capable of anything.

"*Jeff Rawlinson*," Jean-Pierre repeated, almost as if he were reciting a mantra or a magic spell. "That's your name, isn't it, *Jeff*? That's who you are, isn't it, Jeff? *Jeff Rawlinson! Jeff Rawlinson!*"

Jeff stared strangely at Jean-Pierre through those terrifying, pupil-less eyes. His cracked and dry lips quivered as he tried to mouth those two words which Jean-Pierre was repeating over and over.

Jeff Rawlinson . . . Jeff Rawlinson . . . Jeff Rawlinson . . .

"Jeff Rawlinson!" he suddenly cried out, in a voice so loud that it drowned out even the deafening rolls of thunder. "I am Jeff Rawlinson!"

He released his hold on Murphy and she broke

free of his arms, the rusty knife thudding to the ground.

"Yes, you're Jeff!" cried Calvin, as Murphy rushed to him and held him close.

He turned to Kim and Maria-Teresa. "And you—you're Maria-Teresa! And you—you're Kim! Listen to us! Remember who we are—who you are! Come back to us! Come alive again!"

Kim and Maria-Teresa began to sway as the wind buffetted them to and fro. Their features betrayed the struggle which was going on in each of them: the battle between their real identities and the zombies which they had been turned into.

"We're winning, Calvin!" said Jean-Pierre. "We're winning!"

Jeff was staggering around now, oblivious to their presence; Kim had collapsed to the ground, and Maria-Teresa was whimpering to herself and hugging the base of the old yew tree by the Rawlinson tomb.

"Come back to us!" yelled Jean-Pierre. "Jeff Rawlinson! Kim Nishida! Maria-Teresa Fernández! Come back to us!

"No!"

Calvin, Murphy and Jean-Pierre all turned to the open door of the Rawlinson tomb. Even Jeff, Kim and Maria-Teresa looked; but they whimpered in sheer terror, as dogs would at the approach of their cruel and powerful master.

"Mon Dieu?" said Jean-Pierre. "It is she! The mambo! Marinette-bwa-chèch! The evil one! The servant of Baron Samedi!"

Calvin and Murphy, however, knew the newcomer by another name.

"Francesca," said Murphy. "Is that you . . .?"

"Oh God, Frannie," said Calvin. "Not you as well . . ."

Jean-Pierre shook his head. "She is not a zombie, Calvin," he said sadly.

Francesca growled at them. "You've ruined my plans, all of you!"

"You made Jeff into a zombie . . ." Calvin said.

"Yesssss!" Francesca said, hissing like a snake. "He deserved it—he said that we were through—he rejected me! For her, for that little tramp!"

"Who does she mean?" asked Jean-Pierre.

Murphy's face was pale. "Oh my God I understand now," she said. "Jeff dumped Frannie and started to go out with Sophie Ashford . . ."

"Yessss."

"You took control of Jeff and had him kill her!" Calvin said.

"That would have been ironic, wouldn't it?" said Francesca, and laughed. "But that wouldn't have suited my purposes. I wanted to see her suffer, see her humiliated . . . like Kim here, and Maria-Teresa . . ."

"But Sophie died!" said Murphy. "She had a heart attack!"

Francesca laughed again. "Jeff pumped her full of tetrodotoxin," she said almost proudly.

"Which gives the appearance of death," said Jean-Pierre. "And which turns people into zombies."

"But that means that she didn't die at all," said

Murphy, horrified. "That when she was cremated . . ."

"That's right," chuckled Francesca. "She was burnt alive. Oh, how I would have loved to have heard her screams as the flames licked around her body! That would have served the little tramp right! She stole Jeff from me! She deserved what she got!"

Murphy shuddered. "But you killed Claire as well! You didn't turn her into a zombie!"

"An unfortunate mistake," said Francesca. "Jeff got . . . 'carried away'. It seems that, of all the tramps he went out with after me, she was the only only one who left *him!* He hated her."

Murphy looked over at Calvin. They both knew which person Claire had finally dumped Jeff for.

What? Calvin couldn't believe what he was hearing. *Jeff Rawlinson was actually jealous of me and Claire?*

"And Kim, and Maria-Teresa," continued Murphy. "You wanted to destroy anyone who had ever gone out with Jeff . . ."

Francesca cackled. "Of course. But there is one person I have left out, one final girlfriend of Jeff's . . ."

She pointed at Murphy, then glanced over at Jeff.

"Kill her."

Jeff began to move towards Murphy.

"*Jeff*, don't do it," said Calvin.

"You are not a killer, *Jeff Rawlinson*," said Jean-Pierre.

Jeff hesitated, and Francesca snarled.

"Then if he won't do it—I shall have to do it myself!"

With a strength born of madness, she threw herself onto Murphy and her hands reached for the Irish girl's neck. Murphy threw her off, and the two of them rolled around in the mud, first one gaining the upper hand and then the other.

"You stole Jeff from me!" screeched Francesca. "You and all the others! I loved him and you took him from me!"

Her hands went for Murphy's eyes, but Murphy rolled away just in time. For a second Murphy was on top of Francesca. The pendant Jean-Pierre had given her, and which she'd been wearing beneath her leather jacket, fell from her neck.

The Damballah fetish was carved out of some sort of stone and was heavy; it was so heavy, in fact, that Murphy had been thinking of giving up wearing it.

Now she thanked God, the *loas* of voodoo, or whoever else might be listening at that moment in Highgate Cemetery, that she hadn't.

She raised the image of Damballah, the great voodoo Serpent God, and brought it crashing down onto Francesca's skull.

Epilogue

Murphy toyed around with her piece of sushi at Tokyo Joe's. Somehow it didn't look particularly appetising any more. She looked at Jean-Pierre, who was already on his second helping.

"But how did she know about the puffer fish?" she asked. "How did she know that the poison from it could turn people into zombies?"

"Her mother was a Nobel prize-winning chemist," he reminded her. "And her father was a zoologist—remember, they had an aquarium at their house."

"And don't forget that with the prize money Frannie's mother took the family on a round-the-world trip," Calvin said. "That could easily have included Haiti. If Frannie hadn't known about the tetrodotoxin before, she would have soon learnt about it there . . ."

"But the whole voodoo thing—leaving chicken carcasses out as warnings?" Murphy continued. "Why bother?"

"That is where I came in, I'm afraid," said Jean-Pierre.,

"What d'you mean?"

"When I arrived at Castlemare Francesca saw

the ideal opportunity to deflect any suspicion away from herself."

"A red herring you mean?" Murphy said with a smile.

"Exactly. What better suspect than a Haitian just arrived from the land of zombies?"

An awful thought struck Murphy. "So Chippenham . . ."

"Another decoy, I'm afraid," Calvin said. "Frannie had Jeff kill Chippenham and steal the exam answers."

"And when I got top marks . . ." continued Jean-Pierre.

"I know: people suspected you," said Murphy. "We all did—I'm sorry . . ."

"There is one thing I don't understand, though," said Calvin.

"And what's that?"

"When the ambulance came to take Jeff away his body was crawling with worms and maggots. Just as if he'd really been dead . . ."

"So?"

"Maggots live on dead flesh," Calvin pointed out. "Not on living flesh. Jeff and the others might have been zombies but they were still alive."

"That's right," said Murphy, even though she felt her stomach heaving. She put down her chopsticks.

"I can explain that," said Jean-Pierre. "Francesca had stuffed the pockets of Jeff's baseball jacket with rotten, maggot-infested meat, to complete the illusion of his having returned from the dead."

Murphy shuddered. "She must have been really

sick," she said. "What's going to happen to her now?"

"Probably locked away for a long, long time," he said.

"And what about Jeff and Kim and Maria-Teresa?" asked Calvin.

"They will be all right," Jean-Pierre reassured them. "It will take some time and a lot of therapy and counselling, but eventually they will return to normal." He winked at Calvin in an attempt to lighten the mood. "Although I think that Jeff is going to think twice about asking a girl out for a date again!"

"Yep, Calvin," said Murphy. "It looks like the field's finally clear for you, lover boy! Here's your chance to prove yourself, once and for all, the stud of Castlemare!"

"Hey, you really think so?"

Murphy sighed, and looked at Jean-Pierre, who grinned.

"You know something, Calvin, you're never going to learn!" She stood up. "C'mon, guys, let's go and get something to eat!"

Jean-Pierre pointed down to their sushi. "But we have plenty to eat here!" he protested.

"Raw fish? Yuk! After the past two weeks I won't be disappointed if I never see another piece of raw fish for the rest of my life!"

Murphy licked her lips. "All I really want now is a big plate of good old-fashioned steak and chips!"

Also published by Boxtree

SYMPHONY OF TERROR

It's the start of a new year at Castlemare High,
and there are new faces and major changes
being made at the school. Even Jo and Doug,
fellow reporters on the student newspaper, are
surprised by the extent of them.
But even stranger things are afoot. A series of
inexplicable accidents have marred the first few
weeks of term. In a school as exclusive and
efficient as Castlemare, what reason can there
be for arsenic getting into the food in the
domestic science class, or the weights in the
gym being dangerously tampered with.
Mysterious and frightening events indeed – but
that's just the beginning.
For then the killings start.